Praise for *The Pinch Hitter*

"In *The Pinch Hitters*, Roger Stevenson seamlessly weaves together historical insight and captivating narrative, offering readers a poignant glimpse of life in a small farm community during the tumultuous war year of 1944. He illuminates a lesser-known facet of the war, revealing the impact of some of the tens of thousands of German military prisoners who provided an unexpected pool of agricultural workers. Along the way, he reveals the color and texture of the South Carolina landscape and tenacity of the human spirit."

—Dr. David E. Shi
President Emeritus and Professor of History
Furman University

"*The Pinch Hitters* engages the reader with deft descriptions of life on a South Carolina farm during World War II. The characters become real as they interface with oft-forgotten farm laborers from a German prisoners-of-war camp. Each chapter entices you to keep turning the page—a great read."

—Angela W. Williams
Author, *Hush Now, Baby*

# THE PINCH HITTERS

# THE PINCH HITTERS

## ROGER STEVENSON

Brandylane
Publishers, Inc.
*Publishing books since 1985*

ISBN (Paperback): 978-1-962416-34-4
ISBN (Hardcover): 978-1-962416-33-7
Library of Congress Control Number: 2024912687

*Designed by Sami Langston*
*Project managed by Jenny DeBell*

Printed in the United States of America

Published by
Brandylane Publishers, Inc.
5 S. 1st Street
Richmond, Virginia 23219

Brandylane
Publishers, Inc.
*Publishing books since 1985*

brandylanepublishers.com

# CHAPTER ONE

The *Times and Democrat*. "Selective Service Bans Delay In Draft for Men 18 to 25 Except In Specific Cases—Ration Talked." March 15, 1944.

Washington, March 14—(AP)—Selective Service tonight prohibited occupational draft deferments for men aged 18 to 25, inclusive, except when approved by state draft directors or when engaged in an occupation specifically exempted from the policy by the Director of Selective Service.

This extended to men aged 23 to 25 inclusive, a policy already in effect for those 18 to 22. . . .

*Farm Work Angle*

. . . War Department officials were reported to believe industrial deferments should be tightened but to be chiefly concerned over the number of deferments in agriculture. About 562,000 men under age 26 have been deferred as farm workers.

Asked whether there was disposition to look into these deferments, Mr. Roosevelt said he would not say they were receiving more attention than those in any other industry.

Deferments for essential agricultural workers were ordered by Congress but Selective Service has some discretion in determining who is an essential worker and recently tightened up its standards in this field.

* * *

"Git outa heah, you yearlings!" yelled the familiar figure as he lifted a shotgun in our direction.

The *Pop! Pop! Pop!* of a Minneapolis Moline and the periodic thunder of dynamite had drawn us out of Willow Swamp, over a hogwire fence, and across a set of rails to a ridge that was being cleared of trees and stumps. Willow Swamp provided a summer-long refuge for Sugarbread and me. A refuge from the toil and heat of the open fields. From Granny Jack. From Mr. Sif.

Granny Jack had been pushing Champ since early in the month to get the terraced acres that surrounded the sharecropper's house plowed and ready for planting. She and others in the area relied on the *Farmers' Almanac* or on signals from Mr. Sif's bones to determine the best time for planting. This year she fretted over putting out cotton seeds so long before the full moon, but the ground was warming, and she wanted to have a show of seedlings by Easter. Both left her with little choice but to plant on the last days of March immediately after the corn acreage was seeded. Getting the cotton up and the bolls fixed before the hottest weather was her first strategy to beat the ravages of the boll weevil. Mr. Sif warned her about March cotton and said he would rather keep his hands in the field on Good Friday and the following Saturday than risk planting against the moon.

Nature was fully awake following an unusually wet but mild winter. Robins had made their appearance but now were gone. A sizable number had been baked into pies by Miz Ellen, who bought the birds two for a nickel in trade at her brothers' store in Neeses.

Robins were rather easy targets, preferring to forage about in open view rather than in the protection of underbrush. Carroll Westberry's acquisition of a BB rifle at Christmas gave him an edge in picking off the slow-moving, red-breasted delicacies. A number of farm kids, myself included, vied for second place with sling shots.

Catbirds were reestablishing their territory. Like other wing-mates, they were equally occupied with ferrying straw and twigs to craft nests in the trees scattered around the farm buildings. They moved about in the low grass, flashing the white markings of their wings to flush insects from their hiding places.

Beyond the fields that flanked our farmhouse, the woods were becoming speckled with the many colors of spring. Day by day the hardwoods had gathered pigment in their race to rival the uniformly rich needles of the loblollies that grew along the ridges. White oaks lagged behind all others, now only showing the malt of freshly unfolding leaves. Trees at the edge of the clearing were hung heavily with clusters of wisteria blooms, their faint perfume painting the air. The white of dogwoods dotted the woods, and patches of underbrush near the creek bed regained their impenetrable tangle.

Before he left for boot camp in the middle of '43, Uncle Harold had taken us to Willow Swamp nearly every weekend. Sugarbread and I had gained enough confidence from these adventures to put behind us the tales of panthers, bootleggers, and prison escapees lurking uncontrolled in the swamp. But our assurance did not extend beyond the cross-swamp fence at the boundary to Edgar Sligh's place. During the prior summer, we'd talked of camping out along the banks, but talking was as far as it had gotten.

"I ain't skeer't t'do it," Sugarbread had boasted.

"Me neither," I responded, hoping the matter would end there. And it did. At least for a time.

Sugarbread and I were born the same year and grew up almost as twins. Doni assisted in my delivery and was pleased that I would be named Will Livingston after my grandfather. Granny Jack midwifed for Doni two months later at Sugarbread's birth. He was the eleventh of twelve that Doni had birthed, separated from the ones who survived by nearly a decade. I was the first—and thus far, the only—child to be born to Granny Jack and Grandpa Will's seven children. All were slow to get started into childbearing, and the war had further delayed any proof of their fertility. All four of my uncles were now in the war effort, three of them on foreign fronts. My mother and one sister were employed in Charleston. Their move to Charleston placed them near the naval base, which was a port of call for my father and uncle, both of whom had enlisted before Pearl Harbor. Only Aunt Mamie remained on the farm with Granny Jack, a circumstance of continual displeasure to Mamie.

Sugarbread and I competed in every aspect of farm life: making the best sling shot or chinaberry popgun, finding the largest arrowhead, climbing the highest in the bullace vines, picking the most cotton.

Willow Swamp offered opportunities for expanding the competition. Who could catch the largest redbreast or catfish? Who could swing the farthest across the swamp on a muscadine vine? Willow Swamp solidified our brotherhood. But here we also depended upon each other. We poled the boat together, we spotted water moccasins and other hazards for each other, we taught each other about the nature surrounding us, we talked about private things.

Our first chance to get to the swamp that year came on the first Saturday in April after seeding the cotton fields. We wondered if the boat would still be where we had stashed it.

Sugarbread and I met as usual at the creek. From the back porch, my route was always the same. A leap to tag the low-hanging limbs of the pear tree, a greeting to the new litter while passing between the hog lot and Granny Jack's garden, a rap against the knotted boards of the corn crib, a catapult onto the tall stump next to the persimmon tree, a race across the freshly turned field to the woods' edge, hesitation and a passing thought while climbing over the mound, and then down the hill to the creek at an out-of-control gallop.

Swollen by the winter's rains, the creek had broken through the center of the earth-and-log dam, recreating its original path. Generations of farm children had come to this place, building and rebuilding, extending and tending a dam of tree trunks and limbs and mud to back up enough water for a swimming hole. Sugarbread and I surveyed the scene momentarily, giving but passing thought to the work that would be required to putting the dam back together before the summer's heat demanded a cooling-off spot.

The sandy creek bed cut diagonally across the farmplace, forced into sharp turns by boulders and banks and tangles of hardwood roots. A swath of woods on each side formed a substantial barrier between the farmhouse and the sharecropper's fence. That separation caused little inconvenience, even when immediate help was needed at the farmhouse. A strong call of *whoooo* from the back porch would usually bring an echo, and before long, a black face would appear from the woods' edge to ask what was needed.

At its entry onto our land, the creek bed was little more than a damp ditch in dry weather. Shortly after crossing the boundary line, however, it came to life as it picked up water from a series of springs that bubbled from its west bank. Grandpa Will had constructed a wooden frame around the largest of the springs when he and Granny Jack came to the land in the 1920s. They built their cabin on the nearest level land and lugged water up the hillside for over a decade before finding time to sink a well adjacent to the house. Until his death, Grandpa Will demanded spring water at every meal.

Our creek was but one of many branches that rambled through the farmlands of upper Orangeburg County and formed the headwaters of the two major trunks of the Edisto River. Willow Swamp collected all the branches around Neeses and carried them through Norway and into the South Edisto. Near Branchville, the North and South Edistos merged into a single great blackwater river, which made its way to the Atlantic between Charleston and Savannah. The dense, unlogged corridor of black gum, poplar, loblolly pine, and oaks of every variety that flanked its banks through the mid-state was joined by giant cypress stands as the river coursed through the Lowcountry.

The lands around the creeks that formed the Edisto had supported generations of farmers, and before them frontiersmen, and before them Cherokees. The woodlands still teemed with white-tail, turkey, opossum, raccoon, and other small animals. Tales of a panther or a bobcat sighting swept through the countryside peri-odically, but no one had ever brought in a trophy to confirm one.

Signs that the Cherokee found the area agreeable could be found everywhere. Flint arrowheads and pottery shards attracted the keen eye in the open land between our house and the springs that had provided fresh water for as long as Grandpa Will lived. Mostly, the relics were chanced upon while ambling through the pastures and trails. They were most plentiful during late spring and early summer, after the soil had been turned bringing them to the surface and runoff from heavy rains uncovered them along the crop rows. A single mound was the most impressive evidence of Cherokee presence on Grandpa Will and Granny Jack's land. It rested just over halfway along the path from the house to Grand-pa Will's fresh water spring. The sloped sides allowed me to reach it's ten foot pinnacle from all directions.

The swamps that fed the Edisto Rivers were stained with tan-nic acid, and the blackwater potholes were rich with redbreasts, jackfish, pike, and cats. The contiguous dense forest gave equal haven to moccasins and moonshiners.

Sheriff Boggs, placated by the occasional measure of a gal-lon of white liquor and short-handed by the loss of men to the war, let the moonshiners be. He and anyone else who cared about the matter either knew who the moonshiners were or could easily find out by tracing sugar and corn purchases from Chaplin Broth-ers' or Livingston's Mercantile. Most of the backwoods stills were small operations producing ten gallons or so per week for local consumption. The few large operations found in the county were owned by prominent persons with means to truck the output to Columbia or Charleston.

During the prior summer, before he left, Uncle Harold had helped Sugarbread and me fabricate a crude flatbottom boat. We had repeatedly struggled through the underbrush along the creek, ferrying boards and tools to the headwaters of Willow Swamp.

Harold had shown us how to seal the bottom with tar and a sheet of corrugated tin. The metal bottom eased the task of sliding our craft over roots and fallen trees and mud embankments.

Only once had the boat not remained where we left it. We later found it afloat in the swamp, let free either by the hands of a visitor to our playground, or by the high water that accompanied heavy thunderstorms.

* * *

This day, we found the boat on a mudbank, tied loosely to the trunk of a gum tree and nearly filled with water. It slid easily over the mud and into the black swamp water.

We poled through the shallows and into the main body of the swamp. Large shafts of sunlight filtered through the incomplete foliage of gums and oaks. The light rippled along the water's surface as the boat flowed over obstructions and shallow areas on its way westward. The water was still cold and stung as it splashed onto our skin. The small perch, which we pulled from several of our favorite potholes, were almost too cold to handle long enough to remove the hooks. As we floated deeper into the swamp, the lingering winter harshness offered the comfort that we would not encounter cottonmouths or other snakes, either in the water or on the overhanging limbs.

Now, as in times past, the swamp closes around its visitors at first, still and quiet like the night, then almost imperceptibly enlists the senses with movement and song and fragrance. Flickering wings carry a pileated woodpecker on a gliding path through the canopy above to the side of a dead tree where it sets about immediately flicking off the bark and hammering holes into the pulp in search of grubs and insects. Small sparrows and chickadees flit about in the underbrush. The clap of a beaver tail in the distance punctuates the rush of water over an obstructing log. Calls, some familiar and others mysterious, come from the darkness ahead and behind.

Every sound demanded an alertness, an investigation, at least in the mind. "I don't want to hear nuttin' I can't see," Sugarbread said as he searched incessantly for the sources of cracks and whistles and cries and barks and echoes.

Downstream, the intermittent din of machinery called us to the hogwire fence that cut across the swamp at the edge of Edgar Sligh's property.

Edgar Sligh had a pathetically distorted face and was widely reported to be as mean as he was ugly. He was a towering and angular figure, substantially stooped from a life of conforming to a world built for shorter beings. He gave the impression of looking down on the world of other humans, a view which did not generally seem to please him very much. The thought of encountering him in the swamp crept into my consciousness at times from its permanent residence in my subconscious. Penny Sligh, his wife, was acceptably homely, a petite lady with a gentle and gracious spirit. Meanness was distant from her every encounter. I doubted she ever had a mean thought.

"Let's go," we said, almost simultaneously.

"We'll be in big trouble if'n Miz Jack finds out," Sugarbread cautioned.

"We'll be in bigger trouble if ole man Sligh finds out," I responded.

We staked our line of small perch at the waters' edge and followed the fenceline to the north side of the swamp and into the pine forest beyond.

"Betcha it's just a bunch o' loggers," I said for reassurance. "Ole man Sligh's probably clearing another pasture."

Farther up the fencerow, we came upon a highland cooter lodged in the third ring of the hogwire. The turtle frantically struggled to get free, sharp claws raking fruitlessly in the yielding leaves and loose dirt below.

Sugarbread touched his cane pole along the richly patterned shell. A quick sideways lurch, and the cooter's curved beak clamped upon the pole, crushing it between two nodes. "Dat's a snappin' turtle!" Sugarbread exclaimed. "If'n he snap yo finga, he won't let loose it til it thundas."

"Who told you that?" I asked.

"Daddy told me," Sugarbread responded as he twisted the cane a bit. "Wanna smash him?"

"Naw, let's leave him till we git back," I suggested.

"But he be done gone."

"He's hung good. If he gits loose, we can track him."

Sugarbread continued to twist the cane until the turtle's beak cut through, leaving the butt still tightly clamped in its mouth. "Bye Coota," we both said as we slipped on along the fencerow.

We broke out of the pines and crossed the single railroad track where it started its downhill grade into Norway. On the ridge beyond the tracks, trees had been cut as far as we could see. A skidder was struggling with the logs, and two bulldozers were pushing up the stumps. Mounds of stumps and limbs smoldered here and there, and clouds of smoke puffed from the periphery. Beyond one mound, a group of men in striped shirts and pants were putting up a fence that extended several feet above their heads.

"There's Mr. Sligh," I said, pointing to a dark form bent over the controls of a tractor hitched to the fencing.

"What he be making?"

"I don't know. But that fence is tall enough to keep in anything. Betcha he's getting llamas."

"Gleep, gleep!" Sugarbread sounded the call we had invented for llamas at play. Llamas had caught our eye as we flipped through one of Uncle Jme's *National Geographic* magazines. We maintained an imaginary relationship with them, hoping that one would show up at the stockyard sale one day.

We lay on the embankment between the railroad and the clearing for a while, taking in all the activity. The bulldozers generated plumes of sparks and smoke. Three men were sinking post holes in the distance. Beyond them, Mr. Sligh stretched a line of fencing behind the yellow Minneapolis Moline as others hammered at staples to secure the fence.

"Le's go ax him what's he makin," Sugarbread suggested.

"You go ask him, I'll wait right here."

"I ain't goin' by myself. C'mon, le's go!"

We popped up from the embankment and made our way over the disturbed terrain, hands in pockets, directly toward Mr. Sligh. As we approached the tractor, he pushed the throttle up, letting the engine idle, and before we could get to our question, the old man was on the offensive.

We no longer considered asking him any questions and bolted from the tractor toward the railroad. Our stumbling retreat through the stump holes and tree limbs accentuated our distress in getting away from Mr. Sligh. Our flight took us across the tracks and well into the pines before we took a glance back to see if anyone might be in pursuit.

We separated at the path between our houses, Sugarbread heading down through the woods and across the washed-out dam, and I continuing along the ridge and through the freshly turned field to our back door.

I could see through the dogtrot the bed of Mr. Sif's pickup.

"It don't seem like a good idea to have them out heah with you and no supavision," Mr. Sif was telling Granny Jack.

"Well, are you gonna plant my fields and weed the crops?" she asked.

"You know we'll help."

"You don't have enough hands to tend your own crops, Sif. I can't let my crops grow over with weeds and rot in the field like last year."

"If you had'na let them boys go off, they'd be plenty of hands heah for you. Now you're left heah with Champ and Doni. Cephas ain't no count at all."

"Sif, I can't change what's gone on. When the war gits hold of a young man's mind, there ain't nothing to do but let''em go. I pray every day that they'll get home."

"I still don't like the idea."

"I hear Edgar Sligh's already been using them."

Now that's different and you know it. Edgar can stand guard over them, and he's got all those yearlings to help."

"Sif, you're jest worrying too much about us. I'm use to working farm hands."

"Well, I'm going to Norway and do some checking before you get into something you can't handle."

"Okay you do your checking, but I'm supposed to let them know something next week."

"You ain't gonna never change," Sif added as he opened the cab door. "You're just a bullheaded ole woman."

Granny Jack appreciated his avoiding calling her "squaw" and pushed the door closed after he was settled behind the wheel. As he backed the truck and pulled onto the dirt road, she returned to the dogtrot opening, where I had emptied my pockets of their treasures onto a shelf—several smooth rocks from the creek bed; a copper feather from a hawk, I guessed; and a rolled-up fishing line and float, which I had retrieved from a pothole.

Granny Jack gave the items a passing glance and went into the kitchen. She appeared preoccupied with the prospect that able-bodied replacements for her four sons might come to work on our farm.

# CHAPTER TWO

*Times and Democrat.* "Mount Vesuvius Spilling Fiery Streams of Lava. Molten Mass Licks At Doors of Third Italian Town As Populace Flees From Menaced Centers," March 22, 1944.

On the slopes of Mount Vesuvius, March 21—(AP, by Joseph Morton)—A glowing avalanche of lava, spilled from the cauldron atop historic Mt. Vesuvius crunched ahead on the lower slopes tonight and licked at the doors of a third Italian town after having all but completed the devastation of two others.

In the van of the molten, gluey mass scrambled a tearful, pitiful army of bewildered villagers loaded down with household goods.

In its wake lay thousands upon thousands of tons of fiery red coals, piling higher and higher over homes and orchards and vineyards.

. . . Over Vesuvius, indulging in its most fearsome eruption since 1872, hung a blackish pall, and the entire Naples area was in a strange twilight caused by a cloud of gray dust. The stream of lava, 90 feet deep at points, sent up flames and sulfurous fumes.

An Italian scientist, Prof. Giuseppe Imbo of the Royal Vesuvius Observatory, reported that he was unable to detect any signs that the lava flow would cease soon. He has been on the mountain since Saturday noon, when the huge crater "blew off."

Rushing more than 200 big trucks to San Sebastiane and Massa di Somma before the lava reached them last night, the American and British armies, the RAF and the Allied Military Government played a major part in evacuating the two doomed towns.

Platoon after platoon of soldiers, including military policemen, entered the area to assist. A food dump was established at nearby Pollena, where the townspeople, all homeless, were given bread, meat, cheese and coffee. Late today the evacuation of Cercola got under way. No casualties were reported.

\* \* \*

Granny Jack's beloved Will had left her in a paradise of their own making. All was as they'd wanted it to be. The three-mile distance from town kept them isolated. Days could come and go without a passing truck or car to stir the sand-clay road that cut across the northern face of their property.

Granny Jack cherished the quietude. Plaintive chants of hands working the fields and the occasional whines of farm machinery in the distance coalesced with nature's rumblings. The song returned every day to say that all was well. Relatives and friends who happened by were greeted with utmost cordiality, but their departure was the most agreeable part of any visit. Whatever work she had in progress—shelling peas, scrubbing clothes, or whatever—usually continued in a visitor's presence.

"I never seen anyone that needed to talk so much," she complained about most visitors.

"And about nothing a'tall," she frequently added.

Trips to Neeses were infrequent. Both the distance and her near self-sufficiency kept Granny Jack away. A couple trips sufficed each season, mostly for fertilizer, seeds, or to settle accounts after the cotton was ginned. Having little regard for most townfolk, she considered them as different from farmers as those who lived in far-off cities. The land was, to her, a gift of unending abundance. The raw tract of nearly 130 acres, irregularly triangled by streams from the north and the east, had come to Will partly through inheritance and partly through barter with his siblings, who preferred life closer to town. Over the years, about half of the property had been cleared, the higher land becoming pastures and fields for growing cotton and corn, and the richer bottom land for truck crops and sugar cane. It had been Will and Granny Jack's intent to clear only the land needed for cultivation and to depend on the land for all their needs. She viewed as inconsequential her establishment of marigolds and phlox along the roadside and her utilization of the sharecroppers' slow time in hauling underbrush and fallen limbs from the woods. The beauty of the land was sufficient.

Mature trees populated a corridor along the streams and several larger tracts along the property lines. She hesitated to cut any trees, remembering the damage left by earlier loggers. After Will's death, Granny Jack had little time to contemplate her lot or to patronize any desire to be with him. There were still seven children at home to raise and two sharecropper families who depended as much as she on an adequate harvest.

One family left soon after the following harvest, drawn by rumors of opportunities in the cities and the uncertainty of future seasons with Granny Jack in charge. They, like many others in the twenties, would be part of the exodus from South Carolina farms that would diminish colored population to a minority for the first time in over one hundred years. The Negro majority had already begun to wane in the early years of the century and was wiped out in the mid-twenties by a strong wave of migration fueled by the devastation brought by the boll weevil and the demand for unskilled labor in the North.

Will had left Granny Jack with a confidence. The symphony of the growing season had been rehearsed year after year. She knew when to plant, when to fertilize, when to lay by, and when to get the harvest safely into the barns. She depended on the moon, the movement of nature, and the feelings of her bones. She was at peace with it all. Days of heavy downpours and sweltering sun brought equal joy to her heart and smiles to her face.

"We have little to do but to get up in the morning," she repeated often, never counting as significant her dawn to dusk contributions to the farm's success.

"God gives it all. Jus' lets us take what we need."

As it was for most other farmers of the region, cotton was Granny Jack's romance. It occupied her attention from the first days of spring until the leaves began to fall in late October. No other fields were so carefully terraced, no other soil was triple plowed, no other seedlings were so carefully protected against competing weeds, no other blooms were so carefully inspected. And to her, no joy was so great as that of watching the bolls spring open, freeing their white loads. The whitening of the fields in late summer signified that the romance was successful and the reward was there for the picking.

If there were ever a problem for Granny Jack, it was the winter months. She suffered through the cold. Winter was a cacophonous interruption into nature's serenade. It shortened the hours of light and forced her inside. It was a time of continual consumption and little production. The fields were brown. Tree limbs were stark, stripped of their color and richness. Nothing justified the freezing of the earth, the loss of color, the departure of the birds, the hiding of the animals.

Champ's family had sharecropped the land since Will and Granny Jack arrived. The two families were equally invested in energies and dependency. All their children had been born there and knew no other place. None had ever ventured beyond Orangeburg County until Melvin was drafted in 1942. Champ gave names to his favorite trees and talked to them in passing, just as he did to the domestic and wild animals. He felt at ease in taking whatever his family needed.

Champ looked after Granny Jack and me just as he did his own family. He checked to ensure the wood stack was adequate for cooking and heating. He never failed to inquire if there was anything needed before retiring late in the day and crossing the creek to his house.

In addition to Champ, three other men watched over Granny Jack. They managed their oversight in different ways and perhaps for different reasons. I presumed that it had been that way since Grandpa Will's death in 1932.

Doc Connor never made an appearance at the farm but rarely missed contact when we were in town. He had a knack of appearing at Livingston's Mercantile whenever Granny Jack was there. He would help to carry purchases to the wagon and then corner Granny Jack for a talk, And he always anticipated my presence by bringing along a specimen from one of his several collections.

"This one looks like there's still blood on it. See those rust stains," he suggested, rubbing his fingers along the ridges of a finely chiseled arrowpoint.

"Wow," I responded, excited by the probability that his arrowhead had once downed a deer, a turkey, or a settler.

"Why don't you keep it?" he offered.

"Do you really mean it?"

"Sure, just take care not to lose it."

It would become clear to me some years later that Doc Connor owed a debt of friendship to Will, dating from their childhood. It would also become apparent that the doctor's wife saw something in his relationship with Granny Jack other than an obligation to a friend being honored.

Doc Connor claimed to be an atheist, as did his only daughter. His younger sister had died in childbirth, and her unsettled husband left their infant girl in the hands of the bachelor doctor. It was a death to which he never became reconciled. How could a just God take away a mother at the instant of birth? The circumstance forced great urgency on his courtships, which in turn had forced several potential partners to eliminate themselves as candidates for instant motherhood.

He settled quickly on Bea Fogle, who adored the infant and readily accepted the responsibility of childrearing. Bea, a staunch Methodist, was deeply concerned about the girl's choice to follow her father's religious inclinations, and even more deeply concerned what adulterous acts the doctor might commit in his freedom from the constraints of Christianity. His access to the bodies of his patients only accentuated her concerns.

Doc Connor rented rooms in the widow Bolin's house which was located at the edge of a pecan grove on the road to the Neeses school for white children. Porches sheltered the tall windows of the house on three sides. Doc Connor and his wife and daughter occupied a majority of the house, as the widow Bolin required only a sitting room, bedroom, and kitchen.

His office was a world of entertainment and mystery for me. Two of the walls were packed to their ten-foot ceilings with books and with boxes of rocks, butterflies, arrowheads, and stamps. A third wall hosted a wide bench and shelves of colorful jars with exotic labels. A single bed and a couple of chairs arranged around a stove set off from the fourth wall completed the furnishings.

Doc's remedies often consisted of a bit of powder from several different jars, mixed on a slab of marble with a pocketknife and neatly portioned out into individual doses, which were wrapped in brown paper, sliced into the appropriate sizes and then folded precisely.

Perhaps Doc Connor found in Granny Jack a like spirit who was uncertain about Christianity. Perhaps he just had simple admiration for her tenacity and toughness. She functioned in a world of farmers dominated by men, giving them all their due, and in her quiet way outdoing the majority. Perhaps he sensed her zest for learning new things. He had made a covert arrangement with John Tindall to deliver his copy of the *Times and Democrat* to her as he made periodic mail runs. He called her attention to articles he found of interest by framing the columns in crayon.

* * *

Uncle Jme was Grandpa Will's youngest brother. Like all four of that generation of Livingston men, his first employment was with the railroad. Because of his leg, he had spent most of his years at the railyard, ultimately becoming stationmaster and telegraph operator. For a few years he also took on the work of coroner. He now served as proprietor of Livingston's Mercantile and until recently had been a representative to the state legislature from Orangeburg County. The latter venture had held his interest for twelve years, during which time he championed the cause of rural electrification. Leopold Jamison, a Black friend since childhood, had accompanied Jme on every trip to Columbia, serving as his valet.

Jme was a colorful, if not compelling, figure in the House of Representatives. He never took a seat but stalked about noisily on his peg, pipe in hand and mouth trailing smoke, engaging in constant banter with the other members.

"When I came to this body in 1929, only one farm in every hundred had access to electricity. That number has now risen to an astounding three percent! At the rate they're moving, one percent every five years, we can expect the private power companies to carry the benefits of electricity to all of our farms by the year 2429, almost five hundred years from now. That's longer than it took for the rise and fall of the Roman Empire.

"Our farmers cannot wait. They should not be asked to wait to have light in their homes, light for their children to study by, light for their safety, light to enjoy the comforts of home—comforts that we take for granted every day. They should not have to wait for power to process and preserve their crops, power to run their saws and drills, power to operate a hundred other machines. They need electricity now to replace the hands that continue to migrate North from farmlands. Our farms are the lifeblood of this state.

"My friends, if you don't get on board, you're gonna see a way of life disappear from this country. We must stem the flow from our farms to the big cities. We must stop the closing of our small family farms. I can't say it any better than Gifford Pinchot: 'We must preserve the farm as the nursery of men and leaders of men that it has been in the past.'

"My opponents charge that rural electrification is just one more socialistic program. Far from it! The farmers are not asking for Columbia or Washington to run up a single mile of line. They're asking for loans to bring electricity to their homes and barns and shops. Their cooperative will return every penny to the treasury.

"Now, let's be clear about who's keeping the farms in darkness. It's the same power companies that ask our protection to run regional monopolies. It's the same companies that pay handsome dividends to shareholders. It's these companies that take big profits in the cities that refuse service to the farmlands. I have to ask how many of my opponents in this body are receiving dividend checks each month from these companies."

Before Jme left the House of Representatives, he would see passage of the Rural Electric Cooperative Act in 1939, but he later became discouraged by the Declaration of War, which diverted power to war industry. Organization of co-ops and progress toward getting electricity to rural areas would have to wait. The farmer's plight was placed on a back burner. He worried now that the fight would have to be taken up again when the war came to a close.

Granny Jack was uncertain about electrification, not sure she would use electricity even if it was brought to the farm. She reasoned that she might let the mysterious power that sang along the lines on tall poles pass her by completely.

"What's everyone gonna do; no wood to cut, no water to draw?"

Leopold often chauffeured Jme but took considerable abuse because of his caution at the wheel. The gear controls on the steering column of his Model A enabled Jme to drive when Leopold was not available. He generally drove through the farmland until he found us—at work in a cotton field, putting up a pasture fence, or cutting firewood at the edge of the woods. There he could visit without leaving the Model A.

Jme had no hesitation in telling various versions of his heroism in the "Wah" that led to his injury. His stories held Sugarbread and me spellbound. We felt, every time, the sting of the bullet and the crushing weight of the fall as he was shot from his mount in the charge of San Juan Hill.

"Never would have fallen off if the bullet hadn't gone through my leg and into my horse's shoulder," he'd say. "Took my leg off right there on the battlefield. Not even any likker to kill the pain."

It seemed no less real to us when, on another occasion, he explained his one-leggedness to a group gathered around the stove at his store.

"Stepped on a mine in Belleau Wood after chasing the Krauts back 'cross the Marne.

Blew the whole thing off, right at the knee," he said. "Carried it with me back to the infirm'ry, but those vet'narians couldn't do nothing. Just tossed it out in the snow."

In fact, Jme had never seen a single day in battle. He had never served in any capacity in any war, his youth having kept him from World War I, and the amputation precluding action in World War II. His leg had been bruised when several bricks were knocked from a scaffold during the laying of the east chimney of Will and Granny Jack's home. He was nineteen at the time. Although he nursed the injury for almost a year, he eventually yielded it to "Doc Connor's saw."

Doc Connor had amputated it as far distally as he thought possible, leaving a stump below the knee which served as a reasonable attachment for a peg leg. After becoming accustomed to the peg, Jme had resisted the necessity for revision of the stump. He stomped about on the peg and used it for myriad purposes. It served as a handy surface for striking matches, tapping ashes from his pipe, and keeping the rhythm to music. But Jme's penchant for dancing and partying brought considerable abuse to the stump, ultimately requiring repeated amputations of ulcerated and gangrenous tissues. Now only a stub of the thigh remained, leaving Jme dependent on crutches for ambulation, a circumstance he tolerated poorly. In the process, the pain associated with infection and surgery left him dependent on opiates, which were supplied freely by Doc Connor.

Will and Jme had grown close after the chimney incident. Will felt responsible because the injury had occurred during work on his home, although he had nothing to do with the accident. Jme had come to live with Will and Granny Jack for a time. But eventually, his love for town life and his marriage to Minnie Grayson occasioned a permanent move to Neeses.

Neeses was better suited to Jme. He was a Saturday philosopher, alternatively holding forth from the front porch of his mercantile store or the stoop of Rush's barber shop.

Jme took a contrary stand on any issue into which he could draw a combatant. Perhaps he used them to hone his skills for debate in the Legislature, perhaps just to enliven the encounter.

As owner of Livingston's Mercantile, the major source of supplies for the farm, Jme was in position to assist Granny Jack by way of extending credit and securing needed provisions. Granny Jack insisted on paying exactly what everyone else paid and took the same terms of credit as the other farmers on Jme's books. On occasion, Minnie would hold back certain bags of seed if she thought the pattern was one that her sister-in-law would like. These bags were the major source of cloth for conversion into dresses for Granny Jack, her daughter, Mamie, shirts for me, and undergarments for all.

* * *

To me, it appeared that Sif Tyler was the most attentive of all to Granny Jack. He owned a farm twice the size of ours about halfway to town. He gave all appearances of being prosperous, best indicated by ownership of a yellow Minneapolis Moline that provided power for many tasks that, on our farm, were performed by mules or by hand. He also had a Chevy pickup and a variety of wagons which were especially useful at harvest. He had not completely abandoned mule power, though, retaining two teams that he worked alongside the tractor. He preferred mule-drawn plows for gardening and for laying by cotton.

All the same crops were grown on our two farms except for the peanut acreage, which Mr. Sif planted, and the patch below Champ's house we reserved for sugar cane.

Mr. Sif was, to me, a giant prehistoric bird, balding over a ridged crest, greatly beaked, surveying the world from a beady perspective, eyes sunken well behind overgrown brows. His features fell away from a central dominant tether, the whole presentation tan and speckled and thrust forward on a leathery stalk.

I saw him covering the land with all creatures searching for safety behind rocks and foliage. Sugarbread and I labored to find a name for him to use in private—goose, beak, buzzard, limberneck—but none captured his essence in a sufficiently derogatory manner to suit us.

Mr. Sif had his own way in doing everything. Hog troughs had to be built in one design; fencing had to be stapled according to a fixed sequence. Even wood had to be split on precise angles.

"Who built these jack-leg troughs?" he complained once, after inspecting the handiwork that had consumed Uncle Harold and me for a half day.

Mr. Sif assumed general oversight to make sure all went well on the farm after Grandpa Will died in 1932. But he and I never had a particularly good relationship. He felt responsible for the success of the farm and for the well-being of Granny Jack and never hesitated to hand out instruction and punishment for me. Incident after incident formed a gulf between the two of us and too few episodes built on our mutual interests.

For a time, when I was younger, I was inseparable from Granny Jack. I accompanied her everywhere, usually clinging to a leg and never more than a few feet away. Efforts to separate us caused substantial stress, at least for me, and extraordinary resistance.

On one occasion when Mr. Sif attempted to take Granny Jack to inspect the crops without me, I'd pitched a rock that shattered his pickup window. He bolted from the driver's seat, the engine still running, and chased me around the house. I found security against the chimney where Prince was tied up.

"Sic him, Prince!" I urged. Prince strained at the chain, his teeth flashing, and his growling brought Mr. Sif to a halt at a safe distance.

"C'mon here you little towhead. I'm gonna tan your hide!" he'd commanded with a promise I had experienced before.

"Prince will eat yo' hand off if you touch me."

"I'm gonna do more'n touch you," he promised. "You gotta come out sometime."

I'd sunk back against the chimney, sensing for a moment security and protection over the situation.

Upon returning from their inspection, Mr. Sif had again ambled around the corner, this time with considerable deliberation. I remained nestled against the chimney, and Prince greeted him with a snarl. He never paid me my due for that day, but for some time after, I kept my distance whenever he visited.

If Mr. Sif lacked my adulation, he certainly had the respect of the town—landowner and sharecropper, Methodist and Baptist, white and colored. He was known for his square dealings, for his religious convictions, and for his hard work. Hard work was one of the areas which brought the two of us into conflict. My chores were set out by Granny Jack and never were overwhelming. Bringing in water, slopping the hogs, cutting wood, seasonal work on the crops. All told, my obligations could be compressed into the morning hours and a few minutes in the afternoon. During the summer, tomato packing, cotton chopping and picking, and corn pulling were full-time jobs, but ones that lasted only a few weeks at a time.

The balance of time, I was free to explore the fields and woods in the company of Sugarbread or more distant neighbors.

That my every moment was not occupied at some purposeful task was viewed by Mr. Sif as a sin. And he took it upon himself to assign me extra work at every visit: clearing the hedgerow between the pastures, cutting dead limbs from the peach and pear trees, re-nailing tin on the barns, knocking down wasp nests.

To this day, if I find a peaceful minute and sink into some comfortable place, the man maneuvers his way into my consciousness to steal my tranquility. He bashes at my love of contemplation . . . and my attachment to procrastination.

"A boy needs time to explore," Granny Jack would say when Mr. Sif lay out an unending list of chores for me.

"Let'em explore on Sadday or Sunday afternoon," he retorted. "He oughta use these God-given days to accomplish something!"

Mr. Sif's failure to instill the work ethic in his youngest son, Alec, only increased his resolve that I would be "wuth something." He loathed Alec's attachment to music and his frequent escapes into town to play backup on the slide guitar in sessions with his friends.

Mr. Sif was as important to Granny Jack as he was a nuisance to me. Rarely would a week pass without his stopping by to check on her well-being. He shared the bounty of his garden. He provided wagons to haul cotton to the gin. He helped with the hog butchering every winter. His house was always a convenient and hospitable resting place on the way to town.

Miz Lillian, Mr. Sif's second wife (by rumor), was a pleasant and lovely Christian lady. Rarely had I ever seen her outside her home. She played the piano and sang beautifully and occupied a substantial part of her time doing small pieces of needlework that adorned every table and ledge in the house.

Miz Lillian never found it convenient to accompany Mr. Sif on trips to our farm and always appeared gracious in receiving Granny Jack into her home. If she was ever uneasy about the relationship between her husband and Granny Jack, she never let on.

# CHAPTER THREE

The *Times and Democrat.* "Federal Supreme Court Reverses Ruling of Past. Holds Negroes Have Right to Vote In Texas Democratic Primary Elections—Roberts Dissents." April 4, 1944.

Washington, April 3—(AP)—The Supreme Court today upset a decision of nine years' standing and ruled that Negroes have the right to vote in Texas Democratic primary elections, prompting Justice Roberts to protest that the tribunal's opinions are getting to be like a railroad ticket good only for one day on the train.

The eight-to-one decision, stating that "the great privilege of choosing his rulers may not be denied a man by the state because of his color," overturned the Court's unanimous opinion in 1935 sustaining the exclusion of Negroes from participation in a Texas Democratic primary.

The decision has far-reaching implications for the South, where success in a primary is usually tantamount to an election, but whether it will lead to any great increase immediately in the number of Negro voters is considered doubtful. The decision does not touch upon other barriers existing in various parts of the South, such as poll taxes, educational tests, etc. . . .

*Reaction:* Columbia, April 3—(AP)—The Negro

Citizens Committee, a state-wide organization to promote negro interests, looked upon an opinion by the U.S. Supreme Court today that negroes were entitled to vote in Texas Democratic primaries as the "go signal" to file a complaint in federal district court here to seek the same privilege for Negroes in South Carolina. . . .

The rules of the Democratic Party under a section dealing with qualifications of its members limit membership to persons who are "white Democrats."

One party member who declined to be quoted by name said the party had been able to control its primaries in the past and should be able to continue its control, despite the Supreme Court opinion. . . .

In Mississippi, however, Chairman Herbert Holmes of the Democratic executive committee declared: "We still have a few state's rights left, and one of our rights is to have Democratic primaries and say who shall vote in them. The Supreme Court or no one else can control a Democratic primary in Mississippi."

Georgia's state Democratic committee chairman, J. Lon Duckworth, argued that the Supreme Court's action "is not a decision affecting the Georgia primary," and added: "I would say the Negroes are not qualified to vote in the Democratic white primary of this state."

Florida's Democratic committee chairman, Tom Conely, declared: "We'll certainly resist, if possible, any attempt to have Negroes vote in our primaries." He added hope "that the Court's decision won't have any effect in Florida. . . ."

Rep. West (D-Tex) said, "I don't think the Supreme Court has any more right to say who can vote in a primary than it has a right to say who can belong to a church or lodge."

\* \* \*

Henny came to us in April. He and three other men tumbled from the canvas-covered bed of a black Dodge truck that stopped under the edge of the canopy of the large evergreen oak beside Granny Jack's house.

"Norway Branch Camp" was stenciled beneath ten-inch letters: "PW" on the truck door. The same letters marked the canvas above the truck bed.

Henny was the second in an irregular line, which formed alongside the truck.

"This heah's Wolf. He knows 'nough English to git by for all uv'em," said the driver, a sturdy but much older man who spoke as if he knew Granny Jack. "Anything you need to tell 'em, he can do it fer ya."

"Welcome, Wolf," Granny Jack greeted Wolf with assurance, stepping close and extending a strong hand.

Champ leaned motionless and silent against the rear wheel of the wagon. The mules twitched their ears, swished tails, and stamped feet to scatter the flies. Mamie, Granny Jack's youngest daughter, peered from behind a lace curtain in the front room off the porch.

Prince was uneasy, alternating fits of growling and barking with pacing back and forth at the end of his chain. For brief moments, he lay quietly with his attention focused on the gathering in the front yard. He then returned to his repertoire of barking, growling, and pacing.

"Hush up, dawg!" Granny Jack snapped over her shoulder.

"Henny—he's new," the driver continued. "Got hisself captured in Aferca. Can't say's I know any mo'n that. Jus' got here two days ago. Already picked up that shiner since then. Jus' lemme know if he causes any trouble."

The driver continued along the line, giving names and little else, "Enno, heah, and Willi." None of the men spoke except Willi, correcting his name to Wilhelm.

Sugarbread and I stood side by side, silent until Granny Jack had greeted each man. I juggled our version of a baseball, an uneven sphere of tightly wound string, as I stared at each face in sequence. Again and again, my eyes returned to Henny, only to see him glance away.

There they stood! Prisoners of war, each with a yellow "PW" emblazoned on the front and back of his shirt and britches. Golden-haired, tall, straight, young, and as deeply tanned as we would become by midsummer. All except Wilhelm, who was neither tall nor tanned, a bespectacled man inches shorter than any of the others. Nonetheless, he seemed to fit in the group.

These were the men who had the countryside abuzz with apprehension and outrage. These were the very men that some predicted would free themselves and scatter through the countryside, violating the women, pillaging the farms and towns, and threatening the usual serenity and security.

These were the men who brought to the minds of the oldest residents the indignities imposed on them during their youth. They retained the memory, now embellished and imperfect because of the intervening years, of a prior enemy occupation. William Tecumseh Sherman and his Union army of some sixty thousand soldiers and cavalry had created a ten-mile-wide wasteland on their march north from Savannah. They had lingered between the two branches of the Edisto for a while, mapping out the siege on Columbia while recovering from near defeat further south, brought on by an unusually bitter and wet February.

It was this pause that gave General Kilpatrick's cavalry the opportunity to swing west to feign an attack on Augusta and, in the process, torch the town of Aiken. It was one of the few incidents surrounding Sherman's march through the Carolinas that residents enjoyed retelling. Confederate cavalrymen under the command of Joe Wheeler had received sufficient forewarning of Kilpatrick's plans to secret themselves along the side streets in preparation for a surprise greeting once the Union forces were inside the town. Wheeler's men had attacked from both flanks, and the resulting skirmish was considered by locals to be a total rout of the blue coats.

An elderly resident of the outskirts of Aiken testified that Union forces had paraded past her home heading into town early on the morning of February 11, 1865. By midmorning, "the whole caboodle of 'em, with Little Kil at the head," were galloping past her house in retreat "as fast as old scratch would carry 'em!"

The fracas could have resulted in complete defeat and capture of Kilpatrick's cavalry had the trap not been sprung prematurely by volleys from the Alabama contingent. The wild and undisciplined clash that ensued was later recounted by one Union sergeant as "a crush of horses, a flashing of sword blades, five or ten minutes of blind confusion, and then those who have not been knocked out of their saddles by their neighbor's horses, or have not cut off their own horses' heads instead of their enemies', find themselves, they know not how, either running away or being run away from."

As important as it was to the honor of the Rebel defenders, the victory at Aiken was of no ultimate consequence. Within a week, Columbia would be in flames, her homes and shops looted of everything of value, her institutions devastated, and her women and children—white and Negro alike—thrown to the mercy of a Northern entourage delirious with victory and alcohol.

While only a few old-timers remembered any details of Sherman's occupancy, a greater number remembered the harsh years of aftermath. The matter of Yankees on Orangeburg soil—and in a conqueror's role—had never found any measure of acceptance to local folks, nor to South Carolinians generally. The slow recovery from the ordeal, complicated by a chaotic government in Columbia and a hoard of carpetbaggers, had only fixed even more their distaste for the "Nawth." Nearly every farm in the county had sons who had joined the Confederate army, and with few exceptions, every farm had sons that never returned from war.

Now those same farms were heavily represented by sons on the battlefronts in Europe or the Pacific and by daughters assisting the war effort in some manner. The prospect that many of these sons also would not return weighed heavily on the thoughts of their relatives.

For over two years, the Department of Agriculture had been under mounting pressure from farm groups to find replacement labor as able-bodied men left the farms to join the war effort. Still, to many, particularly those with sons on foreign fronts, the possibility that prisoners of war would be sequestered in the area was an outrage! It was inconceivable that the authorities would allow them outside of heavily guarded stockades.

The wage issue was particularly irksome. POWs without rank were paid eighty cents per day plus an additional allowance for tobacco, toiletries, and the like. Officers received salaries based on rank and in keeping with the Geneva Convention of 1929, and they were not required to work unless they requested to do so. The wage was more than that paid to colored farm labor and nearly equal to that of the average US soldier in combat.

Although the diminishing labor force at home had reached crisis magnitude, and although the use of POWs for labor was the obvious solution, authorities were reluctant to accept that solution. They were fearful of the repercussions for American POWs held by the Germans, concerned that the POWs might sabotage their work efforts, and uncertain about what locals might do to the POWs. Only in the fall of 1943 had the War Department, the War Food Administration, and the War Manpower Commission agreed on the mechanism by which POW labor would be made available for farms.

I had heard bits and pieces of the talk about POWs coming to work on the farms but had remained indifferent to the issue. Now with them standing in plain view, any ambivalence disappeared.

Here were the uncles I missed so profoundly. Here were the makings of half a baseball team (and maybe even a Mort Cooper or a Ted Williams in the bunch). Here were bold bodies that could hang onto the mules at full gallop. Here were giants who could stand behind the barn, take a heavy swig of corn liquor, and bellow forth a burning "aahhhhhhh!" Here were men.

"They got their sacks for dinner," the driver interrupted my fantasy. "Let 'em get water from the well."

"I ain't gonna set out no rules. Jus' work 'em like yo' niggas. You have trouble with any one of 'em, and he won't be back."

"I'll drop 'em off here by daybreak and pick 'em up 'fo dark.

After you knock off, jus' let'em wait around till I get heah."

The four men were motioned up into the wagon by Granny Jack. Champ took the reins and moved out toward the cotton field. Sugarbread and I raced behind the wagon and scrambled aboard the open tail. Henny extended a hand to pull me aboard.

Champ's silence was uncharacteristic, broken only by an occasional "Move on, Pearl," and a slap of the reigns against the hindquarters of the two grey mules. Missing were his intermittent fits of unbridled soul lamenting some earthy exigency or pleading for heavenly intervention. There was no greeting to the hawk floating above. No banter with the blue tick hounds that ran alongside the wagon. All was uncomfortably quiet.

"You chop cotton befo'?" Sugarbread asked of no one in particular.

"Ve have not seen cotton," Wolf responded.

"It ain't hard. Jus' leave a few stalks between each chop and make sho they ain't weeds," I reassured.

"The old hoes' the goodest ones," Sugarbread added, pulling a well-worn hoe from the stack in the wagon. The blade had been worn down to half its original depth and all four corners were rounded from years of filing.

As we passed Champ's house, all was quiet except for Tunia, Sugarbread's three-year-old niece, who was playing under the porch.

"Doola bug, doola bug . . ." she sang. She stirred a small stick slowly in the dusty cones that pocked the dirt bed under the porch. "Doola bug, doola bug, ya better come out or ya house'll burn down." She glanced at us as the wagon crossed the front yard and turned beside the house and into the field, then returned to her work. "Doola bug, doola bug. . . ."

Doni and Cephas were some distance down their rows when we reached the field. They stood up momentarily, glanced our direction, then bent back over to regain the *chop, chop, push a weed; chop, chop, take a step* rhythm that propelled them along the row.

Champ appeared content to let Sugarbread and me demonstrate the technique and rhythm to our new recruits while he unhitched Pearl and Queenie from the wagon tongue and led them to a tree at the edge of the field. Sugarbread and I stayed in the middle of the group. Champ's skill carried him away from us. In no time he was alongside his wife and son a couple hundred yards ahead.

"Who's the best slugger?" I asked to a series of quizzical faces.

"Slugger, you know—" I indicated by tossing up a rock and swinging into it with my short hoe.

"Ve play football," Wolf responded.

"We play football too, but you can't play football this time of year. Ain't you never played baseball?"

"Ve play football," he stated again as I tossed up another rock and pelted it toward the mules.

The rows that trailed behind the four Germans held an unacceptable disturbance of the cotton seedlings. The flanking rows that Champ's family had taken were regularly patterned with three seedling hills separated by weedless, hoe-width intervals. The seedlings and weeds they removed lay withering in the middle of the furrow. The rows that Sugarbread and I chopped appeared only marginally better than the rows the four worked on beside us.

"Champ's gonna get our skin," I warned, noticing the contrast of our rows to his.

As Champ's threesome passed us from the opposite direction he stopped, dropped his hoe along the furrow, and walked over to the middle of our group. Champ stood silently for a moment, sweat dripping from gray stubble on his chin, then took Enno's hoe, and with unerring chops and pushes established a pattern in a ten-foot stretch ahead of the group.

Saying nothing, Champ placed the hoe back in Enno's hands and returned to his own row. Doni and Cephas had stopped only momentarily to watch, and now were working their way rapidly away from us.

"Move on along, you two!" Champ yelled back at us as he picked up his hoe.

On the next pass, Doni offered that the work of the Germans

was becoming acceptable. She failed to comment on the rows Sugarbread and I were chopping. Champ passed in silence.

Rows of cotton seedlings greened the fields around Champ and Doni's house. They stretched in all directions, each row separated by a two-foot furrow. A wagon trail leading from the house created an irregular wrinkle between a twenty-acre western field and a slightly smaller eastern patch. Except for a couple acres for gardening, mutton corn, and a low area for watermelon and cantaloupe, all the open land in view of Champ's house was reserved for cotton. The sandy soil on the gently sloping acreage was well-suited to cotton and had become the center of the farm's enterprise.

When at some distance from the clump of POWs, Doni and Champ filled the air with song.

> "Swing on down heah, Jesus
> Swing on down heah, Lawd.
> I be right heah waitin;
> Til ya come to carry me home."

Late in the morning, the field became quiet except for the clucking of a turkey beyond the cotton rows. A couple of turkey hens kept watch from the dry camouflage. Champ encouraged them to stay on the farm by spreading corn along their foraging path.

The red-tailed hawk, known as "coppa" in Champ's nomenclature, floated and banked, his speckled breast and neck sparkling as he surveyed his territory.

Granny Jack rang a bell to signal us field hands at noontime. The midday break lasted about an hour and a half and ended at her discretion when she pulled the bell again. Most workers took about thirty minutes for lunch and an hour for a rest period. Older folk usually shed part of their clothes and napped in bed. The rest dozed against a tree trunk or stretched out on the porch.

Our German workforce stayed in the field, relaxing in the sun alongside the wagon.

Sugarbread and I grabbed biscuits and a couple pieces of fatback from the kitchen table and rushed out the back door of the sharecropper house.

"Where you chilluns going?" Doni questioned.

"Back to the field," I answered.

"Take these jars up the hill and don't you bother them men. They need to eat and rest. Jus' give 'em the water and come on back."

"Yes'm," Sugarbread and I responded in unison, despite having no intention of being separated from the men. "We ain't gonna bother 'em."

Henny walked to Pearl and Queenie, who were tied at the edge of the field. Sugarbread and I trailed along behind.

The two steel-grey mules powered the farm's plows and transportation and were Granny Jack's pride and joy. She had picked them at auction in Springfield and had contracted at the same time to have a large wagon built for them. Except for a few plowshares, they represented her only major purchases since she had been left in charge of the farm. Henny slapped Pearl on the hindquarter solidly. She gave little response and continued chewing on a mouthful of fresh weeds. Muscles along her flank rippled and her tail swatted at the yellow and black flies that provided a constant annoyance in an otherwise lazy and peaceful situation.

He pulled his hand along her back, patted her neck and then her muzzle.

"Can you ride her?" I asked, holding imaginary reigns.

"Nobody can't ride her," Sugarbread interjected. "Daddy done been throwed off, an' Cephas too." Henny continued to talk to Pearl in German, patting her neck and pressing his chest and face against her muzzle. She seemed too occupied with chewing to object to his approach. He leaned against her side and with his arm let a little of his weight be felt. She stomped a back hoof and jerked away from Henny's weight.

He returned to her muzzle, stroking and talking.

"Do you think you can ride her?" I asked again, anxiously, not knowing whether he understood any of my words.

"Ja, Ja, I think," Henny responded.

I wanted him to do it right then.

He untied the rope to Pearl's bridle and pulled her away from the tree.

"He's gonna do it!" Sugarbread exclaimed.

Henny led her about in the clearing between the woods and the cotton field. He pulled her up whenever she attempted to grab a mouthful of weeds. After he circled a couple times, he retied her next to Queenie. He pulled a handful of lespedeza and cupped it to her mouth, patting her nuzzle and neck. Then he turned to rejoin his coworkers.

"Ain't you gonna ride her?" I asked. "I want you to ride her."

"Nein. . . ." He hesitated. "Nein," he repeated.

At the end of the day, the four men stretched out in the wagon for the ride back to the main house. After jumping off the side of the wagon, Henny eased alongside Pearl, patting and rubbing. He rubbed her nuzzle and, with a pat on her neck, murmured, "Tomorrow."

As the men waited for the POW truck, we again took up the matter of baseball. Champ had hewn a hickory bat from the trunk of a small sapling and cured it beside the hearth throughout the early part of the winter. He had carved crude initials W H L on the stock and gave it to me from his family at Christmas. Last summer's baseball had been repaired with new string wound over the old core.

After I demonstrated with a few pitches to Sugarbread, Henny and Enno joined in. Wilhelm and Wolf sat on the ground and rested against Uncle Harold's '36 Ford under the magnolia.

Henny's first attempt was cross-handed and awkward, and contact produced only a slow dribble across the yard.

"Try left-handed," I suggested to the puzzled novice. "Left-handed," I repeated, rotating him 180 degrees and placing his left hand forward on the stock.

"Links, ja," he agreed. He took the next pitch with a solid crack that popped the ball over the yard and into the barn lot.

"Wow!" I congratulated. "That would be a homer."

A smile broke across his face as he relinquished the bat to Enno, who found more comfort batting right-handed but had less immediate success in contacting the ball.

\* \* \*

Our batting practice resumed every day after work, with all except Wilhelm taking a turn batting and fielding the hits barehanded.

Henny's right eye appeared less swollen than when he had arrived the prior week, but the bruising extended from the brow across the cheekbone. I pointed to his injury one day as we waited for his transportation. He pounded his fist into an open palm several times indicating its origin, and then passed his hand across the bruised area to assess the degree of damage.

"Vill be okay," he said, nodding his head in a way I took to mean that it was not severe. I knew that it would heal quickly.

Every weekday afternoon the truck with "PW" stenciled on the side rattled up the road, and our four POWs joined others already on benches in the bed. The truck always pulled away toward Norway with a cloud of dust swirling behind. Every time the dust cleared, I wondered if Henny would return.

# CHAPTER FOUR

The *Times and Democrat*: "Western South Carolina, North-east Georgia Lashed by Night Tornado in 100-Mile Path." April 17, 1944.

Greenwood, April 16— (AP)—At least 12 persons, four of them children, were killed and approximately 200 others hurt when a spring tornado ripped through Greenwood and Abbeville early today, but many others miraculously escaped serious injury as the storm unroofed and heavily damaged Greenwood's city hospital.

Two Red Cross nurses' aides were badly hurt, however, when the wind smashed the top floor of the two story nurses' home adjoining the hospital.

Red Cross headquarters said eight of the dead were in and near Greenwood and four at Abbeville, 14 miles east of here near the South Carolina-Georgia border. Four of the victims at Greenwood were Negroes. . . .

More than 50 residents of Greenwood and Greenwood County were injured severely enough to require hospitalization. A steady stream of men, women and children poured in and out of the badly damaged hospital. All who were able were evacuated either to their homes or to the National Guard armory, while the most seriously hurt remained on the first floor of the debris-littered institution. Miss Mozelle Wiggs, assistant superintendent, said all but two small wards were destroyed. In the confusion no one was able to say how many patients were in the hospital at the time the storm struck.

Col. Oliver H. Stout, commanding officer of the Greenville Army Air Base, ordered all facilities of the base, and its branch field at Greenwood, placed at the disposal of hospital authorities here, and sent an ambulance and several medical corpsmen to assist in treating the victims.

Military police and State Guardsmen maintained an alert and constant patrol of the damaged area, and Boy Scouts, Red Cross volunteer workers, including the Motor Corps, and city official and civilian defense personnel helped with the rescue duties.

Property damage, unestimated, was considered high in the widely-scattered communities that were struck after midnight....

\* \* \*

Breaking ground marked the end of the period of rest the land had enjoyed through the winter months. Only a few rows of greens were kept during the first few months of the new year. Turning the rich earth brought the well revered promise of new life and plenty.

Champ had already broken ground behind the main house for Granny Jack's garden and had made several turns around the perimeter of the cornfield when the bus released me to a weekend free of school. Turning the cornfield always initiated a season of discovery. Its sandy soil held Indian treasures, which were brought to the surface by the iron blade. Champ occasionally spotted an arrowhead unearthed by his plow and slid it into his pocket as a reserve in case my search failed. The most productive times to find arrowheads and fragments of pottery was after a heavy downpour, which scoured the surface of the artifacts and left them perched atop dirt pedestals.

Pottery never interested Champ very much. Collecting pottery discouraged me as well. Over the years I had collected thousands of shards and could never match the pattern or texture of any two pieces. I cared little about the utility the vessels represented or about the artistry that went into their making.

Arrowheads were an entirely different matter. They could not be tossed away or casually slipped into a pocket without examination and reflection on the stories they held. Each point demanded an assessment by the finder's fingertips, retracing the routine of the maker's touch, judging the fineness of the tip, running along each facet of the cutting edge, measuring the flare of the butt and the subtlety of the groove by which it was once bound to an arrow shaft. Smaller, delicately chiseled points were especially demanding. I could imagine a Cherokee father in the light of a campfire, surrounded by sons of several ages, cleaving a broad flake from his favorite master stone, chipping away at the edges until his fingers were satisfied with its form and weight before lashing it to a dogwood shaft in preparation for the morrow's hunt. I could hear him tell of the perfect point that felled a dozen fleeting prey before sailing beyond his vision. The thought returned each time a beautifully balanced point came to my hand.

The March winds tempered the season and mixed budding fragrances with the ever-present aromas of the pig pen and barn lot. The laughter of young calves and mixed rumblings of other spring litters were broken only by Champ's encouragement to the grey mules.

Nothing seemed to compare with romping across newly turned earth, bursting fragile clumps, and forcing cool dirt between my toes. Champ pulled up his mules on the near side of the field and waited with good-natured beckoning until I could reach him.

"Git out heah, boy," Champ's voice rolled across the tilled field and echoed back from the barnside. "How you 'spect to git this field done befo' sundown de way you move?" He knew he'd get the field plowed and I did too, but I liked the importance he gave to my help.

"You find any arrowheads?" I questioned Champ hopefully.

"Ain't see'd none yet. They'll be some befo' we'se through." His reassurance was enough for the moment.

In previous years Champ took the time to make one round of the field with me sitting on the plow handle's cross bar. That perch placed me close enough to get whisked by the mule's tail as it searched for spring flies. Plowing produced a music of its own with the mule's intermittent snorts, the traces rubbing along massive flanks, the cutting of the blade through the firm earth, and Champ's "Gee-heah, mule!" to counter a wayward inclination.

"Look like you done growed too much to ride de plow. Take dese lines and see if'n you kin handle da mule 'round the next row." Granny Jack considered her pair of grey mules to be the best plow animals in Orangeburg County. After several unsuccessful attempts to ride them, Champ had announced, "They ain't fit fo' nothin' but mulin'," and resigned himself to using them only for plowing and pulling the wagon.

After Champ gave me the lines, Pearl picked up her pace as I tried to balance the plow. The first hundred yards overwhelmed me with the complexities of breaking ground. More than two hands were necessary to manage the plow lines, keep the handles straight, and the blade angled to run at the proper depth. For my size, walking to the left of the blade on unplowed surface, to the right on freshly turned clumps of earth, or in the narrow furrow between, posed three equally unsatisfactory options. Pearl showed no intention of helping my predicament and stepped lively, diverging repeatedly from the cut line ahead of her and requiring harsh corrections from Champ.

As we continued along the bottom some distance from the house, Champ burst into song in imperfect time with the rhythm of Pearl's movement. His powerful voice dominated the air and distracted a bit from my continuing difficulties behind the plow. I was used to the mellow chant of his voice heard from across a field. Up close, each word pleaded with intensity.

"Lif' up yo' hands Great Moses man
Won't you lif' up yo' hands fo' me
Dese hands'll keep a working
Pas' de sun gone down
If you lif' up yo' hands fo' me."

"Won't you come off de mount'n
Great Moses man
When de sun gone down
And my work be done
Won't you come off de mount'n fo' me."

As we reached the origin of my irregular course around the field, Champ took over the lines to straighten out the damage and I walked behind, now more intent on finding arrowheads.

"Champ," I inquired, "did you ever see an Injun?"

"Your grandma says dey was Injuns what used to live down next to the spring. I spec' dey been long gone from heah. I don't rightly know dat I'se eba see'd ah Injun. Other'n Miz Jack herself, dat is. And she only be a small part."

The subject of Indians had never been pressed further than that. I had been satisfied to believe that great hordes of Indians lived on what became our farm and for some mysterious reason had strewn the fields with arrowheads and broken pots. The mound had provided a site for endless hours of play. Cowboys or Indians shot from its pinnacle to tumble into the cornfield; kings of the mountain toppled from their thrones and wrestled to the dungeon below.

* * *

Granny Jack had grown up in the western section of Choctaw Indian Reservation near the banks of the Canadian River. Although diluted now by some measure of Caucasian blood, her face still acknowledged her Choctaw heritage. Her skin hung in a loose puddle of wrinkles from heavy cheek bones, hiding almost nonexistent lips. The leathered brown of her skin could have been by blood but was, in fact, from years of exposure to southern sun.

The Canadian River had posed an impasse to the progress of AB & O Railroad as it crept westward. The river's formidable current probably also accounted for the growth of a small frontier town on its east bank. The townfolk had become accustomed to the presence of the AB & O men by 1897. It was their third year there. The framework of the first bridge the men had lashed together washed away in the spring flood of 1896 before any track could be put in place. Granny Jack suspected that only this act of God prevented sabotage of the AB & O's bridge by the crew of the Kansas Rail, which was attempting to cross the Canadian farther north.

The Collins had liveried horses and kept a small boarding house next to their stables. Neither enterprise was very profitable before the AB & O settled in. The loft of the stables was occasionally used by members of the Dalton Gang, who rarely paid their hosts in money, and few other paying customers traveled to that part of the country.

The paychecks and rowdiness of the railroaders had temporarily converted the Collins' community into a boom town. Entrepreneurs chased the men's earnings. The parlor of the boarding house became a favorite place for the workers to drink and gamble. A few young women migrated in from the panhandle to assist the men in the enjoyment of their time away from the rail. Small gangs from as far away as Texas and Kansas periodically tested the security of the bank and the railroad office. Hangings at the end of the street distant from the livery stable, while not routine, became all too familiar for the residents who had known the quieter frontier life only a few years before. The disharmony had become so great as to lead Enos Collins to issue a proscription to his four daughters, which demanded avoidance of the Saturday street scene and limited their contact with the railroaders to serving their tables at the boarding house. Jackie Collins had honored neither restriction.

The summer of 1897, Granny Jack's eighteenth, was the last she would spend in the Indian Nation. She had watched four men hang earlier in the year: Eben Strange for raping the preacher's wife; two brothers named James and Joab Barkley for stealing horses; and a full-blooded Choctaw, only known as Dusty, for his part in a barroom brawl. She had romanced with two AB & Oers before she met Will. She left with him before the winter blizzards began, settling briefly in Wichita Falls and then moving east to New Brunswick and eventually to the small town of Neeses, in South Carolina.

Although they had spent over ten years together, Neeses was the first place they could call home. In Wichita Falls and in New Brunswick, they had lived in railroad cars parked with others on side rails, frequently moving from one locale along the tracks to another. Even the shack that they occupied during the last years in New Brunswick was accepted as temporary.

During the first winter in Neeses, Will felled several acres of tall pines and dragged them along Hard Labor Creek to the sawmill. The lumber would be used during the next summer to construct a two-story dogtrot house. The dogtrot design had been a favorite in the early settlements, the passageway through the middle of the house opening the interior to take advantage of air movement during the hot summer months. The passageway seemed of equal practicality as a shortcut from between the front and back yards and a place that kept mounds of junk from the weather. Dogtrot houses largely disappeared from the landscape once rural electrification brought ceiling fans to stir the air.

Will wanted the dogtrot to replicate his birthplace in every detail. Jason, a younger brother, set aside his bitterness over splitting up the land to assist in drawing the plans, in selecting the best site, and in the actual construction.

Jme, the youngest of the Livingston brothers, had the least interest in the project. He was sixteen years Will's junior, the only child fathered by the Colonel following the war. He had not seen the original house and considered Will's obsession about reproducing it a bit maudlin. Nevertheless, his talent at laying brick and constructing chimneys that drew properly necessitated his involvement. Progress on the house hit snags only when Will and

Jason recalled details of the original house differently. A porch stretched across the entire front of the house with columns of solid heart pine, squared without any taper. The columns were scored along each corner just as the originals to suggest that they were fabricated from four finished boards. Massive brick chimneys stood at each end and a smaller one was placed at the back to serve the kitchen. All bedrooms except Will and Jack's were on the second floor. A living area occupied most of the first floor to the right of the dogtrot.

Uncle Harold's upstairs room was my favorite. From its back windows I could survey the front half of the farm, and during the winter I could see through the woods to Sugarbread's house. It held a special attraction to me because you could get to it by stairs in the dogtrot, and it was one of the two upstairs rooms with its own fireplace. The roof over Harold's room now had a loose sheet of tin that flapped during thunderstorms.

That room also had the best window for throwing out cats. Sugarbread maintained that a cat would always land on its feet regardless of the position or height from which it was thrown. It was easy to get to Harold's room and toss a cat to test the hypothesis without being seen from the rest of the house. Each of the cats from the barn had been tried several times before they learned to keep a safe distance from us. Sugarbread had been right in all the tests. Even the tiger-striped tomcat that we rotated forty times in a rabbit box before flinging him from Uncle Harold's window landed on his feet and wobbled off.

The period of construction had brought Will and Jackie into friendship with Sif and Lillien Tyler, who had recently purchased a farm about halfway into town. That friendship would prove very helpful to Granny Jack in the years following Will's death. Sif would also provide a father figure for the kids left behind by Will. He would over the years imprint them with a confidence in their ability to accomplish any task they wanted or needed to do, and in their ability to do it with the tools available, a philosophy more practical in those years of hardship than Will's more romantic approach to life.

Children came late—not by design but by misfortune and Granny Jack's inability to keep a pregnancy past the fourth month. A girl baby had come shortly after the move to New Brunswick but was lost in her third summer to the malaria that ravaged coastal residents. Granny Jack, too, suffered the fevers of malaria during the years in New Brunswick. Will thought that to be the reason his wife could not bear children, and this as much as anything had decided the move to Neeses. Through it all, Will and Granny Jack were devoted to each other, learned patience, and became careful observers of the manner in which others handled their personal burdens and fortunes.

The countryside around Neeses was well drained into tributaries leading to the north and south branches of the Edisto River. Few mosquitoes inhabited the farmlands around Neeses and the only malaria in the area was brought by the coastal dwellers who came inland for the summer months.

Granny Jack had seen ridicule of the Indians in her hometown and experienced it herself while in Wichita Falls. The folks at Neeses had no experience with Indians and most who called her Squaw Jack had no disparaging intent. She'd returned to her home along the Canadian only briefly in 1907, when Oklahoma was accepted in as the forty-sixth state of the Union. She grieved the loss of her mother in the summer of 1910, before they were fully settled in Neeses, but had to leave the burial affairs to her three sisters.

Will and Granny Jack's move to Neeses was rewarded with an end to their childless home. The decades ahead would bring five boys and two girls. One son died of scarlet fever in late infancy.

Their land was one fifth of the holdings of Colonel Livingston, now divided in equal shares to his survivors. This was the first division of the original land grant received by John Livingston, who had migrated from Pennsylvania in search of a less harsh winter and a longer growing season. In each intervening generation, the full acreage had been passed intact to the eldest son.

The original homeplace was gone. The land lay squarely within the swath between Savannah and Columbia that took the brunt of Union destruction in the spring of 1865. Feints toward Charleston and Augusta had pulled the few Confederate troops from the interior to fortify these cities, leaving virtually no resistance, save the peskiness of snipers, to Union movement. That January's cold and constant rain kept the soldiers mired down and brought supply wagons to a temporary halt, providing greater obstacles to the poorly equipped and dispirited Confederate soldiers.

The Union's four corps and one cavalry division had slugged through the sparsely populated farmlands and forests, sacking the scattering of small towns and disrupting the railroads that linked eastern Georgia with the sea. The region was not without some riches, much of it recently gained as valuables from the coast transported to the interior for haven when residents anticipated Sherman's attack to be along the Beaufort—Charleston—Georgetown corridor.

Officers from one Union brigade had occupied the main house, allowing Minnie Livingston, Jason, and his younger sister the use of one fireplace-warmed parlor. The entourage remained for two days, treating their wounded and their morale, and at the same time consuming the available firewood, food, and livestock. Minnie had feared that the house would be burned when the troops left. The officers, however, thanked Minnie for her "hospitality," wished for her the safe return of Colonel Livingston, and ordered their men on toward Columbia, leaving the main house, the barns, and the slave quarters stripped of their stores but standing.

The last of the Union brigade were barely out of sight when the bummers descended, sacking the farm in search of missed food and valuables, and torching the buildings. The bummers included Union soldiers that lagged behind the major units and un-enlisted tagalongs intent on leaving nothing of use for the Confederates. They'd left as abruptly as they had appeared, anxious to stay in the shadow of the Union forces as they pushed toward Columbia. Their appearance had come so quickly that Minnie had not yet sent Jason and the slave women to retrieve the two milk cows and staples that had been staked out deep in Willow Swamp. This good fortune, and the help of friends whose places were missed by the troops and the bummers, helped Minnie hold the family together until the Colonel returned after the Confederate surrender.

For the most part, the Livingston descendants had since abandoned the land, taking work in the towns of Livingston, Neeses, and North and building homes there. The Colonel's eldest son, Jason, had remained on the land, built a new house with barns and stables, and successfully farmed the cleared acreage. He held the land intact until 1907 when the Colonel's widow died. Her death had embroiled the family in a hassle that never subsided. Jason was the most bitter. He'd held the land together and provided for Minnie during her widowed years while the rest of the family adventured elsewhere. Splitting the land into five equal shares, one for each of the Colonel's surviving children, was a travesty of justice that he never got over. Will's arrival with his wife and children, to claim his portion of the land so soon after Minnie's death, did nothing to ease and encourage a reconciliation.

From the beginning, Will's dream of rebuilding the original home had to be abandoned. The homesite was on Jason's share of the land and was now occupied by a simple farm home perimetered by a cluster of willow oaks.

The 130 acres Will sectioned from the eastern face of the estate would provide well for his family. It was crossed by two creeks, and a series of springs at the head of one branch provided an immediate source of fresh water. A few acres had been cleared and fenced by Jason and his children. Clearing, fencing, and planting consumed Will until his death in 1932.

* * *

My disappointment at not spotting any arrowheads on the last turn around the field vanished as I saw Sugarbread emerge from the woods beyond the field. I ran across the field to share with him my new information. "Champ says that Injuns lived down next to the spring and they buried all the dead Injuns at the edge of the woods." We were both caught up with the same anticipation as we raced toward the mound. Indians buried everything with their warriors. Tomahawks, bows and arrows, everything.

# CHAPTER FIVE

The *Times and Democrat.* "Major Leagues Begin Season This Tuesday. Third War-Time Campaign Open Under Complications." April 17, 1944.

New York, April 16—(AP)—Unruly spring training weather that washed out many final tune-up games, plus a trickle of returning ball players, whose draft and war job status have been changed serve to further complicate the third wartime major league season that opens Tuesday under an unofficial nod of approval from the White House.

Vice President Henry Wallace will sub for FDR again in tossing out the first ball at Washington when Clark Griffith's highly-regarded Senators pry off the lid with the Philadelphia A's. Other openers in the American are New York's world champions at Boston, St. Louis at Detroit and Cleveland at Chicago. . . .

With all lineups liberally sprinkled with rookies, managers had banked heavily on the final weekend of exhibitions to give them a starting day lineup, but most of them will have to experiment as they go along.

In many ways the opening weeks of the season will present another phase of training activity with one vital difference—this time it counts. At least 10 of the 16 big league clubs are not set in vital positions and the others would like some more time. . . .

Now that the President has given his blessing—through Secretary Stephen T. Early—on baseballs' continuation, all that is needed is a similar vote of confidence from the fans in opening day turnouts. . . .

Of the 474 players under contract in the big show, approximately 40 per cent are 4-F and the same percentage 1-A, on call or subject to induction. The other 20 percent is divided among those with military discharges, under 18, over 38 and Cubans not subject to the American draft for six months.

\* \* \*

Several circumstances contributed to the closing of school early in the spring of 1944. The unusually wet and cold winter months had taken their toll on the untended clay roads, making the school's only bus undependable even when gas was available. Neeses owned a road scraper, but it had remained parked in town ever since John Whittle had enlisted in the Navy. Mr. Sif, in part annoyed by the recurrent necessity for extracting the bus from the ditch at the bottom of Tyler's hill, had convinced the School Board that keeping school open "jus' for the yearlings" was an unnecessary expense.

The school at Neeses for white students was an imposing structure and a source of considerable town pride. Located just beyond Fulmer's pecan grove north of town, it was the community's only two-storied brick building. A series of wide steps led to the colonnaded entrance and wide, planked oak hallways. Eleven grades were housed in the single building, with each grade except the first sharing a room with an adjacent grade. An ample auditorium on the second floor accommodated all town meetings, and most outdoor gatherings were staged from a detached wooden lunch house placed forty to fifty yards from the main building.

Most farmers saw advantages in enrolling their children through the first several grades, during which they learned to read and write and handle figures. After these initial years, many children were removed for much of the fall and spring months for use as farm labor. If they returned to school at all, it was during the winter months, and then merely as a diversion.

A clapboard schoolhouse had been built about a mile farther out of Neeses for colored children. The single large room with potbellied stoves at each end served all grades. Colored students were not allowed on the school bus, and few families had any means of transportation other than by foot. Those who lived on farms more than a couple miles from the school had little chance to attend. Sugarbread was among that number.

The high school grades had been stripped of their older boys, a few to bolster the local work force but the majority gaining premature entrance into the military as soon as they acquired facial hair or counterfeit documentation that they were seventeen.

Mr. Sif had noted to the School Board that the younger kids had proven their worth in the fall harvest of cotton and corn.

"They can be of greater help now in plowing and getting seeds in the ground. Greater help to their families and to their country," Mr. Sif had successfully argued.

Miss Hattie Padgett was the only person to put up much of a fight before the School Board. The old maid had devoted her life to teaching fourth and fifth grades, advocated for a full eleven years of schooling for every child, and opposed every effort to shorten the school year. It was in her grades that class size began to dwindle, a phenomenon that townfolk attributed to excessively vigorous curriculum, homework requirements, and rigid discipline.

"This war will come and go, just like the last one, but the need for education will always be there. I cannot believe you would even consider closing the doors of this school. Why, we hardly have these children half of the year as it is." Miss Hattie had complained since the war began.

"I've been teaching at this school for fifteen years, and I've never so much as been late a single day to teach these children." she continued.

"Miz Hattie, why don't you be late for a few days?" Mr. Sif had suggested, to the amusement of the board members. "Why don't you just be late!"

I found the same delight as the other pupils when the school closing was announced. However, I saw no particular benefits for family or country as Mr. Sif had suggested. The lengthening days would bring ample time after farm chores were completed for trapping and hunting and other springtime pleasures. It would be no time until fishing and swimming were my daily preoccupations.

We had certainly felt no great stress to survival since the war began. There were fewer mouths to feed in our house and in the sharecropper's house. Fewer acres of all crops except cotton were planted, and Champ was able to keep up with the plowing of these reduced acres. A work force of Granny Jack and Doni, Champ and Cephas, and Sugarbread and me, seemed fully adequate. In fact, the four allotment checks received each month from Granny Jack's sons were stacked in the hall closet awaiting their return.

Granny Jack had never appeared anxious about her loss of labor to the war. Although her sons had taken over a large share of the farm work in recent years, she managed now without them and knew she could continue until the war was over. She had known hard times before and was tempered for such circumstances. Will had been gone since '32, leaving to her the responsibility for the farm, the sharecroppers, and seven kids, with only two of them old enough to contribute substantially. Champ's family had given faithful support year in and year out.

Champ's children had known no other home, and he and Doni resisted the urge that had overtaken fellow tenants to move to a city up north. Champ felt the burden of the war as well, with Melvin and Junior, his eldest sons and best workers, in the army. He was able to get some work out of Cephas, but that was unpredictable. It had been necessary for Champ to take Cephas down beyond Macedonia Church to see Wartman Watson on three separate occasions during the past year. Wartman had received Cephas with full confidence that he could be free of his fits as the devil was driven from his body. Wartman had this power, the same as his mother before him and her father before her. As far back as ancestors could be recalled, the power had descended through alternate sexes. Watson's family lore placed the original power in experiences of a boy purchased by John Watson from the slave boat *Horizon*, which had anchored in Charleston Harbor in 1796.

Wartman, or at least his power, was blamed for most unexpected happenings around Neeses, especially those which could not be laid by irrefutable link to one of the town pranksters. He received his share of praise as well, usually stemming from augmented testimony following the resolution of some malady. The breadth of his power saw little bounds. Over the years he garnered notoriety for halting the growth of tumors, talking the fire out of burns, drawing the soreness from festering wounds, halting hemorrhages, and endless other successes. He even cured Benjamin Cribbs, who'd once hiccupped for eight days straight.

Wartman's greatest notoriety lay in the ability to remove warts, and for good reason. Like him, the forebearers of his power removed warts, but none were known to have assumed them into their own bodies as Wartman did. It was rumored that Wartman's mother had been found to have warts scattered over her torso as she was being prepared for burial. In fact, it was that finding which planted the seed in Wartman's mind that the power he and others before him possessed must function by the transfer of another's problem to his own body or consciousness.

Whites and colored of all ages from Orangeburg and neighboring counties came to Wartman: women with warts in some delicate location, farmers with warts that were constantly irritated by plowlines or work implements, and kids with warts anywhere.

The extent of his work's success had only become externally obvious in recent years. He was now covered with warts of various sizes, extending from the crown of his head to his palms and soles. Even the warts had warts, some hanging like limp drumsticks as large as those from a spring fryer. Nothing obscured the great proliferation of warts. Nor did Wartman try, often working in his fields stripped to the waist or carrying on business in town, seemingly blind to the attention his appearance demanded of children and adults beyond his acquaintance.

Wartman professed to know the source of each wart. "Dis one heah come from ole Mr. Bolin's head. Don't rightly know why it settled heah."

He'd acquired several from my left thumb that were alive and well on his chest. One from Sugarbread's knee was next to mine.

In his early years, Wartman had used his powers to cure animals and humans alike, but with confirmation in his mind of the mechanism by which his powers worked, he later came to deny animals access to his power, fearing that he might assume some unacceptable animal feature. Granny Jack lamented the expected loss of Wartman's power for the future. He'd failed to marry in his younger years and now his appearance foreclosed that option.

The devil resident in Cephas, being resistant to coaxing, had been driven from him on the three occasions he was given over to the care of Wartman. Each time, Cephas and the family returned home elated in anticipation of freedom from the spells that had destroyed his confidence and limited his usefulness since childhood.

But still, the fits returned when he became excited or overheated in the fields.

It was hard to imagine that Cephas had Champ's blood. Champ was a tall and sturdy man with large muscles and shovels for hands. Cephas's gaunt face and wiry frame was marked with thick dark scars, ravages of his seizures. At a distance he appeared as old as Mr. Sif, stooped and slow. For days after a seizure, his speech remained slurred and painfully deliberate.

Champ and Doni cared for Cephas tenderly, saving for him the tasks he could manage, protecting him from cruelties that might occur at gatherings, teaching those things he could learn, celebrating his every accomplishment, and surrounding him with love. They accepted that his childhood would never end and praised their God for bringing Cephas to them.

\* \* \*

Neeses, a place of multiple personalities, held a town grant dated 1903, although the community had thrived as Silver Springs for a number of years before that date. In 1893, the community of 110 men, women, and children residing within a half-mile radius of the springs had submitted a petition to the state requesting designation of townhood.

A bed of boiling springs located about midway between the branches of the Edisto River first attracted settlers to populate the surrounding lands. From colonial days, the water's healing properties had been rumored throughout the state. No doubt the springs had been well known and visited for centuries by Cherokees in their passage along the corridor from the town of Ninety-Six in the upstate to the junction of the Edisto branches some thirty miles farther south.

No records detailed the lives of any settlers in the vicinity of the springs until after the Civil War. A Methodist campsite occupied a number of acres adjacent to the springs for many years, and those who lived close by called themselves the Silver Springs Community. A stagecoach stop and a travelers' house accommodated all who came to bathe in the springs. Water from the springs was also bottled for consumption for its healing properties.

Both the travelers' house and Methodist camp long had disappeared prior to my first visit to the springs. Dense underbrush crowded the trail; only a few of the town's families made regular visits for drinking water.

The center of activity of the Silver Springs Community eventually moved away from the springs to a site one half mile to the west. There, John Neece had sold a right-of-way to the South Bound Railroad Company in 1891. He agreed to construct and operate a stationhouse as part of the deal. Over the ensuing years, stores and houses sprang up along roads flanking the tracks.

The relocated community took the name of Neeses in appreciation of the efforts John Neece had made to obtain a letter of incorporation. It served as the hub of farm activity within a three-to four-mile radius. Trains from both directions stopped every day and their screeching brakes brought life from all directions. Some were curious about who or what might appear on the platform; others came just to view the groaning, puffing behemoth.

There was a single telephone available. Residents preferred the telegraph to send messages too urgent for the postal service. Tillman's store, a small all-purpose shop, dispensed the only medicines available other than those compounded by Doc Connor. During the summer months, Tillman's occasionally kept ice cream.

Shortly after incorporation, Neeses became embroiled in conflict with the county government. Neeses residents complained that all resources of the county were pulled into Orangeburg at the expense of the small towns. The small towns were provided neither schools nor teachers, the roads were impassable in the winter, and the chain gang was used almost exclusively for the upkeep of Edisto Gardens and private homes in Orangeburg. Neeses and the neighboring towns of Sally, Springfield, and Wagener grew increasingly intolerant of the county administration and, in 1907, drew up articles of secession. The new county would be named Edisto. The move was doomed to fail from the outset when it became clear that *both* Neeses and Wagener intended to be the seat of the new county government. The matter was brought to a quick resolution when the mayors of all four towns involved were arrested.

* * *

Since colonial days, South Carolina had placed her economic fortunes in single crops. The cultivation of rice in the Lowlands, flooded by the coastal terminations of the state's great rivers, began to challenge trade as an economic factor prior to the beginning of the seventeenth century. In the following century, Elizer Lucas, a transplant from Antigua, succeeded in growing indigo for the production of dye on a family plantation located near Charleston. The plantation became very profitable in the decades leading up to the Revolutionary War. But the British subsidy and strong prices for the dye disappeared during the war, allowing rice to make a temporary comeback. All the while, cotton struggled to gain an economic foothold.

But later, as the central and western portions of the state became safe, cotton became the overwhelming choice of farmers. Cotton liked the hot weather and withstood the often dry summers better than any other crop. Arrival of the Whitney gin late in the 1700s increased the profitability of the fiber and, in the years thereafter, cotton had no close challenger as the king of crops. Its reign continued through the years of my childhood. Only invasion by the boll weevil in the early twenties—and the subsequent occupation of the state's farmlands by that devastating insect—threatened cotton's preeminence.

The migration of cotton mills from New England to the upstate of South Carolina at the turn of the present century, and the shift of the planters to the long-staple cotton preferred by the mills, had assured a good market.

From March through October cotton occupied the attention of townfolk and farmers alike. Ground was broken early in March as the soil warmed; seeds were sowed before the month's end; seedlings thinned and weeded in April and May; the crop laid by with a final plowing in July. The bolls were dabbed with molasses and arsenic from June until August. There followed a pause during the blistering weeks of August and September while the bolls expanded and burst into white splendor. October was occupied with picking. In a good year, all debt accumulated during the growing season was retired. In a poor year, the debt was carried forward in anticipation that the next year would hold better fortune.

So perfect was the match between cotton and the sandy soil of the state's central counties that few farmers planted any other money crop, although chicken and eggs and vegetables were bartered with neighbors and merchants year-round. Everyone set out a winter garden and raised chickens and hogs and a couple of cows. Mr. Sif planted some acreage in winter wheat and oats. But during the winter our land, like that of most of our neighbors, lay fallow.

Will had found the clearing around Champ's house to be productive for cotton, and Granny Jack was hesitant to rotate the moneymaker to any other location. Each acre usually bought forth about three quarters of a bale. At twenty cents a pound for lint, her cotton acreage allotment brought over twenty-five hundred dollars at Chaplin Brothers, where cotton was ginned for the seed. This represented the total cash flow for the year.

After the second picking, any late-opening cotton was a gift to Champ and his family. If they could scavenge one extra bale, the season's end bonus allowed for new outfits for all the family.

"Ya oughta love cotton. Cotton's put meat on those bones," Mr. Sif often said, as a reminder of the respect I should hold for cotton. In retrospect, perhaps I did. I remember clearly the sense of accomplishment at my first hundred-pound weigh-in. I do not recall whether I ever reached the two hundred-pound-a-day echelon. I doubt it. Lying on the cotton piles in the midday sun, riding atop a wagon packed with cotton heading for the gin, carefully recording the bale weight for Granny Jack—perhaps I did love cotton.

# CHAPTER SIX

The *Times and Democrat*. "Germans Herd Polish Jews for Massacre. Underground Report Few Left Alive by Nazi Masters." April 25, 1944.

Washington, April 23—(AP)—From the Polish underground has become a grim document purporting to show how the Nazi extermination policy has reduced Poland's pre-war Jewish population from 3,500,000 to barely 50,000.

The report, made public by John W. Pehle, executive director of the War Refugee Board, was written shortly after a series of "liquidations" last November.

The underground report—all details concerning it are a closely-guarded secret—said:

"Last month (October) we estimated that there were only between 250,000 and 300,000 Jews left in Poland. It is our opinion that in a few weeks there will only remain about 50,000.

"We want all Jews, and the world at large, to know that our youth nobly defended the life and honor of its people. Since the heroic epic of the Warsaw ghetto we have in recent months written the grand and glorious chapter of the Jews of Bialystok. . . .

"On the fourth day of the action the fight began.

Bloody combats took place in a number of streets. Just as in Warsaw, the Germans entered the ghetto in armored trucks and equipped with field artillery. They brought along about 1,000 gendarmes and SS-men and a number of Ukranian detachments.

"The Jews retaliated mostly with grenades and incendiary bombs. They also had a few machine guns. Several hundred Germans and Ukranians fell or were wounded.

"In order to crush the uprising the Germans did what they had done in Warsaw—they set the ghetto afire."

\* \* \*

Pressures from London for the United States to accept Axis prisoners of war began well before President Roosevelt's Declaration of War on December 7, 1941. The number of Italians and Germans captured far exceeded the capacity of the British POW Camps. The crisis in the British camps notwithstanding, it took nearly one year of additional negotiations before the State Department acquiesced, accepting about a third of the 175,000 POWs offered by the British.

Captives transshipped from Great Britain were but the first wave of POWs to be accommodated on US soil. Those ranks were swollen several-fold with the Allies' success in the North African and Mediterranean campaigns. They poured into ports along the East Coast on every available vessel and were quickly distributed by rail to military installations and makeshift camps throughout the nation. Anxious to abide by the principles of the Geneva Convention, and more importantly to avoid any reprisals against American POWs held in Germany, the War Department made every effort to provide civilly for their new charges.

Camp Charleston came into existence with unexpected suddenness. Two Italian ships lying at anchor in Charleston Harbor the morning war was declared provided the first interred, a contingent of some sixty-two officers and seamen who were to remain in confinement for the duration of the war. A holding area was hastily arranged some ten miles north of the city on the site of an abandoned CCC camp. As it turned out, the site was transformed into one of most acceptable of the permanent POW camps, having barracks instead of tents for shelter, contact with locals of Italian and German ancestry, and access to the culture and entertainment of this most European of American cities.

The Italian POWs used their ingenuity and limited resources to make Camp Charleston even more livable, planting gardens for production and beauty around the barracks, putting up flags and pinups on the walls, and leveling a field for soccer. Five of the twenty available barracks were put into use and provided spacious accommodations. POWs were permitted to furnish the canteen with furniture made from packing crates. Many acknowledged that they probably were living better than the rank of Italians living at home under wartime exigencies. The food and accommodations were tolerable, and daily contact with Charleston locals was the rule rather than the exception.

Work programs permitted a majority of the prisoners some view of life in the Carolina Lowcountry. In private, they decried the positions of the Black field hands. No one at home was treated with such disdain, compelled to work so long and hard in insufferable heat, paid such low wages, and confined to quarters barely fit for animals.

A steady procession of locals, the curious and those involved in some charitable or educational venture alike, filed through the camp every weekend. Camp officials saw no reason for strict regimentation with the seamen, who appeared to be content with being ashore, away from the European theatre, and in some limited contact with the young women who had flocked to Charleston to help in various war efforts.

With the arrival of the first major shipment of POWs in early July, the tranquility of Camp Charleston changed abruptly. The new arrivals had endured a ten-day ordeal of near constant seasickness on the crossing from Algeria on a freighter. A confusing crush of thousands of POWs disembarked at Norfolk and endured the indignities of both delousing and a two-mile march before being herded onto a train headed south. They were suspicious of the colored porters, who supplied drinks and sandwiches. They were shocked by the shanties that dotted the farmlands and lined the dirt roads of small towns along the way.

Although in German uniform, the majority were foot soldiers conscripted from other nations. Major Adams assigned the officers to a newly cleaned barracks and distributed the others among the barracks already in use by the Italian POWs, hoping by that plan for them to become quickly accommodated to their new home.

A day was given to the issuing of clothes, medical examinations, photographing, and a recitation of camp rules. Following a weekend of leisure, a third of the German contingent was assigned to the vegetable fields in the company of the Italians. They were transported through the northwestern edge of the city, past the site of the 1902 Interstate and West Indian Exposition, and across Memorial Bridge to fields west of the Ashley River, a distance of about fifteen miles.

The PW wagons were wooden boxes less than six feet in height mounted on truck beds. Except for portholes in the front and rear for ventilation, they were completely closed in order to limit incidents with the locals and to prevent escape. The black wagons became a familiar sight for Charlestonians, and rarely did incidents arise other than an occasional barrage of angry words or rubbish from teenagers.

Camp Charleston quickly became divided into two camps. The German contingent were rigorously regimented by their officers, while the Italians continued to enjoy their nonstructured camp life. Unrest between the two groups grew steadily over the first week together. Sergeant Bill Stevens, a Charleston native and aide-de-camp to Major Adams, recorded in detail the disruptive events and conversations of the following week.

Helmut Berger, the German officer of rank, registered his displeasure with conditions in camp the week after his arrival. Major Adams stood casually behind his desk as Captain Berger goose-stepped in, unsuccessfully attempted a sharp heel click with his newly acquired camp-issue uniform, and snapped "Heil Hitler!" with an outstretched salute. "I am Captain Helmut Berger, from der—"

"All that's not necessary, Captain. I know who you are. Have a seat," Major Adams invited, motioning to a chair beside his desk.

"I will stand."

"Suit yo'self, Captain . . . hope you don't mind if I do," Adams stated as he sat and leaned back in his oak-slatted swivel. "What may I do for you today?"

"You may conduct this camp according to provisions of the Geneva Convention, sir," Berger began, referring to a page of notes.

Having little knowledge of the convention's provisions, Adams nodded noncommittally and allowed Berger to continue.

"We must be allowed the company of our countrymen. We vould rather to have tents on the ground than to barrack with the Italians. Und second," he continued, "my men will work no more in the field ven it is so hot."

"Is there anything else, Captain?" the Major inquired.

"Ja, the shoes. These shoes are nein good for my men. They have nein click," Berger stated, making only a muffled sound as he sharply forced his heels together. "The convention says you must allow us our uniforms."

Major Adams pulled himself up slowly and, with knuckles against the desk, glared at Berger. "First, my dear Captain, you are a prisoner of war. I will give the orders here and you will obey. If your men wish not to work, they will not eat. If you do not like the boots, you may go barefoot. And if your men do not like their barracks, they may move their cots outside."

"We have got to live here together for a while," Adams added. "You can make it easy on yourself and your men, or you can make it hard. Is that understood?"

"It is understood, Herr Major. My men will move their cots and will not go to the fields."

"As you wish, Captain. You are dismissed."

The hours following were festive as the Germans moved their

cots into the pathways between the barracks. Their stomachs were comfortable from a full Sunday breakfast. Berger moved among his men, ordering the cots to be placed in straight lines and for personal belongings to be stored neatly in boxes beneath the cots.

"Kurt, who waits for you in the fatherland?" Berger called out from a position beneath Major Adams' window. It was the signal for Berger's men to join in one of their favorite drills.

"Mein Fuehrer, mein Stuttgart, und mein fraulein, Greta!" Kurt answered in a spirited yell.

"His Fuehrer, his Stuttgart, und his fraulein, Greta. Heil Hitler, Heil Hitler, Heil Hitler!" The response from the Germans echoed throughout the camp.

"Hans, who waits for you in the fatherland?"

"Mein Fuhrer, mein Bremen, und a keg of beer."

"His Fuehrer, his Bremen, und a keg of beer. Heil Hitler, Heil Hitler, Heil Hitler!"

"Jon, who waits for you in the fatherland?"

"Mein Fuhrer, mein Weimar, und Kurt's fraulein, Greta."

"His Fuehrer, his Weimar, und Kurt's fraulein, Greta! Heil Hitler, Heil Hitler, Heil Hitler!"

The Italians gazed from open windows or milled about the perimeter of the German details, occasionally taunting their comrades. The Italians in Barracks #6 vacated their comfortable home with the Germans, encouraged to do so not out of sympathy but because one of the departing Germans indicated their intent to torch the barracks that night.

Major Adams consulted with General Hayden at Fort Jackson, who agreed that no concessions would be made if a work strike occurred.

To a man, the German contingent refused to board the wagons that would take them to the fields Monday morning. They arose with the Italians at 5:30 a.m. reveille, made their cots, marched to a breakfast of bread and water seated next to Italians with full plates, marched back to their cots, shaved and showered in makeshift facilities, and policed the grounds around their cots.

At 7:30 a.m. they stood fast as the Italians climbed into the wagons and departed.

By mid-afternoon, growling stomachs and stifling heat began to puncture the festive mood with discontent. The second night spent as open feasts for the Lowcountry mosquitoes brought bitter complaints from the Austrians, Poles, and non-Nazi Germans.

Discomfort among the striking POWs grew by the hour, and by nightfall on Wednesday the men talked openly about returning to the screened barracks before the evening descent of the mosquitoes. On Thursday morning, the old camp routine had returned as if the strike had never occurred. Reveille rousted the men from cots that had found their way back into the barracks during the night. At 6:00 a.m., all were enjoying a full breakfast except Berger, who was again standing before Major Adams in the commander's office.

"You may tell your men that work assignments will continue as before. Your men may have canteen privileges in one week if there are no further disturbances." Major Adams avoided telling Berger that concessions would be granted in the months ahead, allowing Germans to be housed together, as well as organization of one of the empty barracks into a gathering hall, complete with a large poster of the Fuhrer at one end.

In time, Camp Croft and Fort Jackson would become the two principal sites in South Carolina where POWs were held. They also served as centers for distribution of a much larger number of men to branch camps—satellites located around the state, convenient to farms or other enterprises that contracted to use POW labor.

By early summer of 1944, Norway Branch Camp had grown into a sizable community. One hundred and thirty men now occupied row after row of tents, and plans were in progress to double the number before harvest time. All were German POWs, the Italians and Austrians being segregated in other locations. To residents of Neeses and Norway, the POW population was a frightful number, since the total Saturday count for Neeses was 215 and for Norway only a few more. Saturday counts included every man, woman, and child who could be found in town on the major day of trade. Full-time residents accounted for only about a third of a Saturday count.

Eight guards were assigned to Norway Branch Camp, providing a guard for every sixteen or so POWs, a higher ratio than was found at many POW camps. Five of the eight were enlisted men, transferred with the POWs from Fort Jackson, and three were local, one for each eight-hour shift.

Norway Branch Camp arose on fifteen acres on the southernmost extreme of Edgar Sligh's land, which extended through Willow Swamp, across the Atlantic Coast Line tracks, and onto higher ground. The entire parcel had been stripped of its cover of blackjack and scrub pines, except for two sizable willow oaks. From its southernmost access, the gently sloping land had been terraced into three sections of roughly equal size. Rows of green tents patterned the first section. The middle section provided a near-level sports field and relief from the summer sun beneath the two oaks. Several piles of partially burned limbs and stumps remained in the lower section, which sloped on to the ACL tracks.

The surrounding fence was constructed much like that of a cow pasture, but with cedar posts jutting nine feet above ground and holding ten strands of barbed wire. Guard towers overlooked the compound from the entrance and from the sides of the middle section. A completely clear strip about fifty feet in width separated the tents and activity areas from the perimeter fence. Posts along the interior of this corridor warned: *Anyone venturing beyond these warning posts will be at risk of being shot.*

Each morning the camp emptied itself into five trucks that crisscrossed the surrounding farmlands. One headed toward Neeses along Route 4, dropping off crews at several farms, and returned toward camp on the wire road. Other trucks distributed workers along the highways that sprouted from Norway toward Springfield, Denmark, and Orangeburg. Only the laundry crew and cooks routinely remained in the camp during the day. They kept the work clothes clean and mended, prepared lunch for the guards, and readied a large supper for the crews upon their return.

POWs were required to wear prison clothes: dark blue britches and shirts, except on Sunday, when they were permitted to use whatever uniforms they possessed upon capture or had been able to barter since imprisonment. POW garments were stenciled in a non-uniform fashion with the large yellow or white letters: PW. Most britches were lettered on the seat, though some were lettered on the fronts and backs of the legs.

In addition to two sets of work clothes, each man was provided with four sets each of drawers, undershirts, and socks, plus a belt, gloves, raincoat, and shoes.

Wages of eighty cents per day were credited for each full day of labor. Payment was made in the form of canteen coupons, in part to reduce the likelihood that guards would be bribed. Farmers who sharecropped were allowed to run a POW labor bill, to be paid at the end of cotton picking. Granny Jack had figured that the total labor bill for the four men who would spend most of April through October in her fields could be paid with a single large bale of cotton.

No high-ranking officers were placed at Norway Branch Camp. The camp was established to provide farm labor, and officers were not required to work. Lieutenant Eberhard Koch was the only resident POW of rank. He was included in the labor force by his choice, perhaps to prevent boredom, perhaps to maintain an easy opportunity to escape should he decide to do so.

POWs were obliged to attempt escape from the stockades, and Norway Branch Camp experienced its share of escapes and attempted escapes. Testing of the caution perimeter was a daily occurrence, usually in the guise of an unintended happenstance during a soccer game. Soccer balls were kicked deliberately beyond the warning posts, and a player would venture into the prohibited area to retrieve it. Such security challenges rarely elicited any response from the guards other than a warning shot as a reminder that the intrusion had not gone unnoticed. Guards and prisoners alike were aware that similar perimeter testing at other camps had resulted in the shooting of POWs by less tolerant guards.

In the early months at Norway Branch Camp, the prisoners often concocted elaborate schemes to get outside the compound. Escape plans often involved the railroad, either making it to a passing train and hitching a ride to some distant unknown place or using the train as a diversion while leaving the camp in another direction. The guards were alert to the attraction of the railroad and shifted their attention to the tracks each time the puffing of the coal engines came into earshot. Only the local trains that stopped in Norway, usually two each day, posed much of an opportunity for escape. The southbound braked as it passed the northern face of the prison on a downhill grade into Norway. The northbound local passed equally slowly as it struggled away from the station and up the incline.

Two men, Gerhard Maier and Joseph Neufeld, did make it aboard a southbound freight on June 6, and were not found to be missing until roll call the next morning. They commandeered an empty boxcar, which, rather than carrying them to freedom in Florida, was detached on a side rail in Norway to receive a load of cotton seed. On the second day of waiting to be recoupled to a southbound locomotive, the two tired of their hunger and loneliness and turned themselves in to a shocked stationmaster, who, after providing them a full meal, drove them back to camp.

Visitors provided additional impetus for the men to find a way free of the barbed wire enclosure. Young women were drawn to the gates by curiosity, a happenstance that delighted the captives and elicited repeated public pleas by Captain Taylor to discourage visitors to the camp's perimeter. More enterprising women found that joining local church groups—which frequented the camp to set up educational programs and a library—was the most expedient way to gain direct access to the men.

The language barrier placed the men under pressure to pursue a more complete relationship. Kurt Trinkaus did leave the confines of the camp—and repeatedly so—over a period of several months. He had struck up a cross-fence romance with Annie Whittle that reached such intensity he decided to risk all to be in her physical company.

Through the services of a comrade in the sewing room, he

acquired a change of PW blues that were reversible, with a plaid shirt lining and a khaki trouser lining sufficient to obscure the white PW imprints. The laxness of the guards and the aid of several of his barrack mates gave Kurt many an opportunity to leave after bed check by slipping out the latrine door and under the barbed wire to freedom.

Once in the woods beside the camp, he would reverse his clothes and walk along Route 4 to Norway and to Annie's apartment. After an evening repast, he would then reverse the process to retake his place inside the compound before the 5:30 a.m. wake-up call. The initial escape proved so simple that Kurt repeatedly rendezvoused with Annie over a three-month period, enjoying the cover provided by his fellow captives. On one occasion he was aided by a sharecropper who transported him to his waiting love in the back of his wagon. Kurt disguised his accent by feigning a speech difficulty secondary to an abscessed tooth, adequately counterfeited with a wad of tobacco in his left cheek.

Kurt might have been able to continue his exploits until the war ended were it not for the jealousy of Hans Palmer, a fellow prisoner, who, lacking the invention and pluck to carry out a similar adventure for himself, tipped off the guards to the tryst one night.

When the guards arrived at her apartment, Annie was noncommittal, she and Kurt having satisfied their passions and Kurt already having returned to camp, passing the guards on the way as they drove into town in pursuit. He was soundly asleep when the barracks were rousted out at one a.m. for a repeat bed check.

Escapes from the compound occurred sporadically throughout the existence of Norway Branch Camp. Once the Germans became accustomed to camp- and work-site routines and more fluent with English, schemes for escape became less complex. In most cases, the prisoners merely walked away from the work site. All escapees eventually returned to camp on foot or in the company of a local or Sheriff Boggs. The hours of freedom were usually spent strolling about the streets of Norway, trying to locate a woman they had met in camp, or wandering about in the woods.

They often made no attempt to camouflage their work clothes, acting as if their activities were part of prison routine.

No charges fit the escapees' actions, since they were neither criminals nor fugitives from justice nor even deserters. In escaping, they were in fact doing that which was expected of prisoners of war. In the end, the punishments handed out were little different from those exacted for violation of the "no work, no eat" policy of labor camps. The posting on the door of the dining hall on April 29 read:

| Kurt Trinkaus | absent from bedcheck. | 7 days confinement on bread and water. |
|---|---|---|
| Erick Stoll Stefan Klein Hans Stauss | field workers, Edgar Sligh's farm, damage to 6 rows of cotton. | 7 days confinement on bread and water, 30 days beer restriction, 30 days canteen restriction, 7 days wage recoupment. |
| Eberhard Lunger | caution perimeter violation, 3rd offense. | 30 days beer restriction. |

I longed for the day when Henny's name would appear on the posting: Henny Stauss, absent from camp, apprehended in Willow Swamp, fishing with Will Livingston.

# CHAPTER SEVEN

The *Times and Democrat*. "Pensive Leads Turf Parade As Champion. Winner of Kentucky Derby Tops Three-YearOlds of Nation." May 8, 1944.

Louisville, Ky., May 7— (AP)—Pensive heads the three-year-old turf parade today because Ben Jones and Conn McCreary, a couple of boys from Missouri, outfoxed all of their rivals in the richest of all the 70 Kentucky Derbies at Churchill Downs yesterday. . . .

All season Jones had been running Pensive in bar plates, both on his hind hooves, because the son of the 1933 English Derby and St. Leger winner, suffers from tender feet. Jones took them off for the first time in the Chesapeake Stakes a week ago at Pimlico but the Calumet chestnut dropped a close decision to Gramps Image.

Plain Ben, although some of the boys insisted today he should be renamed "Miracle Ben," was not strong for shipping the colt to the Downs but yielded to the persuasion of McCreary, who never had been closer than third in three previous Derbies and could well have remained at Pimlico and picked up some $3,000 by riding Wright's Sun Again, winner of the Dixie Handicap. So, Jones took off the bar plates again yesterday and what happened is history.

Somewhere around 60,000 to 65,000 fans will recall how Pensive was all but lost in the pack during the early running, how he ran into a blind switch at the home stretch turn when Mrs. Payne Whitney's Stir Up, 7-5 favorite, and Mrs. George Poulsen's Broadcloth were battling for the lead, and then how McCreary took him to the rail and won by four and one-half lengths. Broadcloth was second a length in front of Stir Up, who once again showed that offspring of Stimulus do not like a distance race.

In taking Pensive to the inside, McCreary caught Woolf and Arcaro napping. Woolf, up on Broadcloth, and Arcaro, guiding Stir Up, were heads apart at the time and apparently had forgotten about anybody else in the race. But even if they were aware of Pensive flying through on the rail, it was doubtful if they could have done anything about.

Picking up $65,200 of the record $86,700 purse, Pensive ran his earnings for the year to $80,925 and gave him a standing of four victories, three seconds and one-third in eight starts. . . .

\* \* \*

Passing over the Kentucky Derby article, Granny Jack labored through every inch of the *Times and Democrat*, concentrating her efforts initially on the articles that Doctor Connor had marked. Evening hours were devoted to the newspaper, a kerosene lamp aglow at her side, and during the cold months, a wood fire warming her feet. For years I fell asleep in a far corner of the large front room to the slow music of her rocking chair, the soft flicker of flames and the murmur of print being ciphered.

Of all the tasks I ever saw Granny Jack tackle, reading was the most arduous. She recognized few words on sight, requiring that virtually every word be spelled out. Each sentence became painfully protracted.

"A s - e - r - v - i - c - e—service c - h - a - r - g - e—charge of t - h - r - e - e—three c - e - n - t - s—cents per c - a—can w - i - l - l—will be m - a—made if the p - a - t - r - o - n—paaytrun b - r - i - n - g - s—brings cans. H - o - w - e - v - e - r—however the c - a - n - n - e - r - y—cannery w - i—will s - u - p - p - l - y—su-pply cans at a c - o - s - t—cost of six c - e - n—cents for n - o—NO 2 c - a—cans and s - e - v - e - n—seven c - e—cents for n - o—NO 3 cans w - h - i - c - h—which i - n - c - l - u - d - e - s—includes the s - e - r - v - i - c- e—service c - h - a - r - g - e—charge."

Until I was corrected by Miz Lane in the first grade, I pre-sumed that the spelling of each word, followed by slow and de-liberate pronunciation, was the correct way to read. After hearing Miz Lane flow smoothly and steadily through the lines of the *Oak Hill Primer*, Granny Jack's reading efforts became something of an amusement.

Her other nighttime routine became an irritation. After com-pleting her kitchen cleanup, she called for her footbath to be read-ied. The job of washing her feet before she attacked the *Times and Democrat* had fallen to me at the age of four. Before then, I had watched Mamie wash Granny Jack's feet and couldn't understand why she objected and searched for excuses to escape her obliga-tion. Initially, I eagerly took on the chore.

Foot washing usually took place at the stairs in the back hallway. The location was close to the door where the water pails were kept and from which dirty water was thrown into the back yard. A white enamel basin accommodated one foot at a time and enough water to cover the ankles.

Foot washing happened when the cadence and exertion of the day began to spiral toward the quietude and peace of evening. The final glow of the sun falling below the horizon of loblolly pines could be seen through the screen door.

It was there that I first heard of the Choctaw Indian Nation, of the Collins' livery stable, and of the Dalton gang. It was there I came to know Grandpa Will, the AB and O Railroad, and the Canadian River. It was there I learned about Striped Hampshires,

White-faced Herefords, Rhode Island Reds, and Seneca Chief. It was there that the markings of cottonmouths and rattlers and copperheads were drawn into my memory. It was there that foam on a dog's mouth and diarrhea in a newborn calf became ominous images.

Granny Jack talked about gnarls in young trees that stunted their growth and forever made them vulnerable to the winds of adversity. Even at my relatively undiscerning age, I knew she spoke not of trees but of people.

Her coarse voice never carried the sting of criticism. At times I find myself engulfed in the search for a hidden spring that has brought forth character or deed, analyzing a circumstance to the last detail, and in the end, remaining ill at peace with why we are as we are and act as we act. Her memory stirs an unrest at such times. I wondered if two generations of dilution of the Indian blood coursing through my veins had weakened my capacity to face life with equanimity.

"I remember it just as clear as if it was yestiday," she told me, of her first encounter with Grandpa Will. "Pappy told my sisters and me to stay off the street that Saturday morning. Three men from the gang that had held up the railroad office and taken the money that had come in to pay the workers who were putting up the bridge 'cross the Canadian River, were gonna be hung that morning. Pappy didn't think it was proper for us girls to see the hanging.

"Your Grandpa worked on that crew, and he was making good money. He came into the livery stable that morning to rent a horse just to run in the hills.

"He was the handsomest young buck I ever seen. I fixed up a horse and led it out into the street where he was settling up with my daddy. Those three robbers was already swinging at the other end o' the street. They stayed up there all day as a lesson to everybody else.

"I waited all day for yo' Grandpa to bring that horse back. I guess he knew from the look in my eye that I thought he was something. He was back at the end of every week after for a horse, and he didn't want anybody but me to get it ready.

"It wudden long before he was pulling outta that place and I was right there beside him. I remember it just like it was yestiday."

My scrubbing continued until the lesson of the day was complete or until I was dawdling in the water. The ritual was completed with application of Watkins drops to her corns and fanning the drops into a hard lacquer.

After I started the first grade, foot washing became a problem. Carrol Westberry and Cal Whittle learned of my nightly duty and spread it over the schoolyard. It gained for me the nicknames of "Judas" and "Water Boy."

*We can't let Water Boy play or he'll be too tired to wash the ole squaw's feet*, was the taunt that brought the matter to a head, engaged me in a schoolyard scrap with Cal, and earned six painful licks for both of us from Mr. J. T. Bonnette's paddle.

For a period thereafter I rebelled against the job, occupying myself away from the house and pretending not to hear her call. I even tried being sick for a couple days—until faced with the threat of a visit to Doctor Connor. Knowing that castor oil was his major remedy for coaxing young patients back to health, I readily abandoned the tactic. Eventually I acquiesced, but never again had the same passion for the exercise as in earlier years.

\* \* \*

After struggling through the farm news page of the *Times and Democrat*, Granny Jack blew out the lamp. The creaking of pine boards traced her shuffling steps across the room to bed.

The springs complained rhythmically as she rolled and shifted but stopped abruptly when Prince began barking. The dark silence of the room was pierced again and again by his sharp challenge.

I could hear a soft voice outside, beckoning to Prince, "Come heah fella, good ole boy, come heah, now." All was quiet again after a moment.

"Miz Jack," the voice was louder this time, and its youthful quality was familiar. It was Sugarbread. "Miz Jack!" the call came again. "This is Sugarbread. Is you awake, Miss Jack?"

"Yeah, Sugarbread, I'm awake. What you doing out there?"

"My daddy want to know if you can come see 'bout Momma. She been trying to have the baby tonight."

Granny Jack did not answer, but knowing she would go, I jumped from my bed to light the lamp.

"What are you doing?" she asked as I began pulling on my britches.

"I'm going with you," I answered quickly.

The rhythm of her dressing changed quickly as she stated her position plainly: "This ain't gonna be no place for children, so you just take off those britches and get back to bed. Besides, you can't be up and around all night, you gotta be in school in the morning."

"I'm still going," I replied, forgetting the usual consequence of doing anything other than exactly what she told me to do. It was probably the fear of staying alone in the big house that made me so firm in my commitment. I don't remember having any interest in seeing the child born. I could tell she wasn't going to take the time to argue about the situation and immediately grabbed the lantern to light the path through the woods.

"Hey boy! You still out there?" Granny called.

"Yas 'urn," Sugarbread replied.

"Go on back and tell Champ to get some water on the stove and I will be right along."

Doni had seemed more tired than usual that afternoon, especially after helping Granny bring in a ham from the smokehouse. Afterward, she'd waited for Champ to hitch up the wagon and left our place sitting on a pile of sacks in the tail of the wagon. During the day, she had worked steadily beside Granny Jack, putting up plum jelly without complaint, alternately humming and singing a few lines of "I Come to the Garden Alone."

The night air nipped a little and my teeth chattered as I trotted to keep up with Granny Jack's determined pace. The lantern threw long shadows away from us, creating figures that moved in the dark woods along the path. There was activity all about us as the frogs croaked politely, one behind the next. A little gust of wind rustled the summer leaves, and an occasional hoot came from deep in the woods.

For a moment all became quiet except for the whistling of my britches as I trotted along. The sound gave me the feeling that someone was close behind, and I kept glancing back.

Rarely did anyone travel the narrow path between our houses after dark. At most, Granny Jack and I made the trek once or twice a year. Back in 1941, when winds from a hurricane ripped the roof from the back porch and left the sheets of tin loose and folded back in several places on the second story, we had run to Champ's home to sit out the night.

This night, Champ's hounds met us before we were in sight of the house, barking like they had treed a possum.

"Shush up, dogs!" Granny commanded. They did not obey but kept out of range, loping alongside us. Another lantern was now just ahead, the sparkling of gold teeth and white eyes unmistakable Champ's.

"Get out de way, dogs!" he roared as he kicked in their direction. "Oh, Miz Jack, I thanks you so much for coming. I be sorta scared all by myself with dis hapnin.'"

"That's all right, Champ," Granny Jack reassured. "How is Doni now?"

"She been having lots of mis'ry since 'bout sundown. She still strong, tho I ain't neber seen her had dis much trouble anytime befo' with no chillun. She act like her pains much worser. I tell you, I think we jus about too old to have this happen."

"Well, she will be all right," Granny comforted. "She ain't no spring chicken no more, but she will do okay."

Doni was lying in the front room next to the fireplace. She was covered with sheets and holding on tightly to the iron bed frame above her head. Her eyes were clinched and her hair was brushed straight up over her head. In a soft, pleading voice she was crying, "Oh my Jesus, help me Lord, nobody knows, nobody knows. Oh, help me, sweet Jesus."

Tunia was sitting on the hearth, Sugarbread standing beside

her, still panting from his run back home and holding his hands out toward the few glowing embers in the fireplace. Sugarbread stuck up one hand and smiled broadly when I came in.

I went to stand beside him.

There was a new odor that night, an odor different from the sweet odor of hairdressing that always prevailed in Doni's front room.

"All you kids get in the kitchen, out the way," Granny Jack ordered. I wasn't sure the command included me, but I went anyway.

"How's that water coming along, Champ?"

"I'll have to check it, Miz Jack. I imagine it ain't had time to bile yet."

"Bring me a pan full of what you got in heah, and keep the rest cooking."

From the kitchen we could hear the springs squeak and the soft voice repeat, "Oh, my Jesus. Oh, my Jesus, I be so weary. Give me strength, stand by my side, sweet Jesus."

Champ stood by the kitchen door, looking into the front room, tears welling in his eyes and dropping across his face as his eyes clinched tightly each time Doni cried out. He fell to his knees and whispered softly, "Good Lord, please hep my sweet Doni. Don't make yo serbant suffa so like dis. She been good to all 'o us, Lord. Please Lord, help yo sweet serbant."

Champ pulled himself up along the door jam, rubbed his eyes on his shirt sleeve, and came over to the stove to check the pots of water. "Now, all you chilluns, you thank the Lord for a good momma, then you lie down heah next de stove and go to sleep."

"Help me with this misery, sweet Jesus," Doni pleaded over and over. Then all became quiet again, except for the logs crackling inside the stove, water boiling, and dogs whimpering under the back steps.

Doni cried out again and when she quieted, Granny told her to rest. "The baby's doing just fine. It's coming down good."

Champ spread a quilt over Tunia, who had fallen asleep. Sugarbread and I remained awake, lying alongside the stove, listening and looking at each other. The monotonous sound of burning wood lulled away any consideration of staying awake until the baby was born. My thoughts drifted back to the bones we had dug into at the mound the previous week. My dream was hardly broken by a baby's cry that trailed into the night.

# CHAPTER EIGHT

The *Times and Democrat*. "Fifth Army Liberates Rome From Nazis Sunday." June 5, 1944.

Allied Headquarters, Naples, June 4— (AP)— Fifth army troops captured ancient Rome tonight, smashing German resistance in the heart of the Eternal City and sweeping on northward in pursuit of battered German forces which had dynamited some installations.

The mop up on the center of Rome—the first Axis European capital to fall to Allied troops—was completed at 9:15 P.M. (3:15 P.M. Eastern War Time) by Americans and Canadians under L. Gen. Mark W. Clark....

A smoke pall hung over parts of the city where the Germans began their demolitions shortly after 3:30 p.m. (The BBC in a broadcast recorded by NBC said this indicated the Germans had "probably destroyed the bridges over the Tiber" river, which runs southward through the city and then southwest to the Tyrrhenian sea. Across the Tiber lies Vatican City....)

Hysterical with joy, Roman citizens at the city's outskirts amid kisses and tears moved on U. S. and Canadian tanks and infantrymen dashing up the Via Casilina and then battering into German defenders holding the suburbs, a front dispatch from Associated Press Correspondent Daniel De Luce said....

This break into Rome, center of Catholicism and once the seat of the ancient Roman empire, came 24 days after the Allies unleashed a powerful combined offensive of the Fifth and Eighth Armies, and 12 days after Fifth Army men on the Anzio beachhead hurled forth their power-drive aimed at the capital....

The great roundup of prisoners continued—with more than 14,000 now taken by the Fifth Army alone. The Eighth Army had captured at least 6,000. Five of the 18 German divisions engaged in Italy already had been virtually annihilated....

\* \* \*

As the weeks passed, handling the mules fell more and more to Henny. Champ fed and watered them soon after he arose each morning and usually had them partially harnessed and tied to the gate before turning to other chores. Henny had charge of them from that point until he turned them back into their lot at day's end.

On the first Friday in June, I asked Granny Jack to allow Henny to drive us to town the next morning in the wagon. Granny Jack had given up driving the mules years ago when one of the previous team had run away with her, lodging her buggy against a pine tree. The buggy was never repaired and rested now in the barn in front of Champ and Doni's house. She talked of using the new mules and wagon for transportation for years after their purchase, but something prevented her from ever doing so.

Mr. Sif had made several attempts over the years to teach Granny Jack the basics of driving his pickup. After acquiring a used '36 Ford, Uncle Harold had tried as well. Although excitement in the household was periodically kindled by the possibility of Granny Jack learning to drive, neither Mr. Sif nor Uncle Harold made much progress. Twice Mr. Sif's pickup wound up in the ditch and required extraction by the team of mules.

Granny Jack took the instruction good-heartedly, except for the ditching—which she blamed on Mr. Sif's yelling at her and grabbing at the wheel. She'd eventually became resigned to the fact that driving vehicles was a task for men. It required too many things at one time.

Only a few of the town's women drove, which they did of necessity. Both Miz Padgett and Miz Lane had Chevrolets. That seemed to be a requirement of bachelor ladies.

"Let's get Henny to drive us, he can do it," I urged.

"I don't know," Granny Jack responded.

"I'll get my hair cut if Henny can drive us," I offered, reversing without thought my long-held position against a barber cut.

"Don't get too excited, but I'll think about it."

"We'll be able to bring everything home right then."

"We don't need much, but I'll think 'bout it," she repeated.

Fatneck Rush's barber shop was two doors down from Livingston's Mercantile in the Bank of Neeses building.

"Now you stay at the front of the line, so we don't have to spend the whole day in town," Granny Jack instructed as she left Henny and me and ambled off towards Livingston's.

As was his custom, Fatneck appeared promptly at ten o'clock, opened the tall wooden doors, and invited us in.

"Mr. Rush, this is Mr. Henny who is working on our farm with us."

Fatneck said nothing but busied himself filling the yellow tonic bottles, arranging towels, and slapping his razor back and forth along the sharpening leather.

He and several of his kin folk had huge, fleshy jowls that flowed into a saccular mass beneath the chin. Unlike his father, who amused the older kids and frightened the younger ones with a repertoire of frog sounds while inflating and shimmying his redundant tissue, Fatneck tried to obscure his tumor behind high-collared shirts. The attempt was successful only in giving him the appearance of having no neck at all.

Neeses Bank had closed in 1931, unable to return any significant holdings to its depositors. Although few people lost any great amount of money in the crash, no one in Neeses had since ventured into the banking business.

Granny Jack had never forgiven Jme about the bank default. It was a family sin under any circumstance, but with Will ill and not to recover, Granny Jack held the loss unpardonable. Jme had anticipated the closing and quietly withdrew his deposits during the final weeks of the bank's operation. His appointment to the Bank's Board of Directors had no doubt provided insight not available to most.

The bank building nevertheless remained a popular gathering site for the white men on Saturdays. They whiled away endless hours playing checkers, reading the *Times and Democrat*, and just telling tales as they waited their turn to be cut, shaved, or trimmed.

The porcelain-armed barber's chair shared the middle of the open room with a cast iron stove, now piled high with old issues of the *Market Bulletin*, the *Times and Democrat*, and *Progressive Farmer*. The teller's cage on the back wall still identified the former occupant.

"Been a long time since I seen you, Will. Your Granny been cutting your hair?" Mr. Rush inquired.

"Yes sir, sometimes. But she wants you to cut it today."

"Well just get yourself up here and we'll see if we can lower your ears a bit."

Henny settled into one of the cane chairs near the front window. John Franklin arrived with the morning's *Times and Democrat*. Mrs. Maude Freeman brought Erick and Derrick, her twins, and was followed shortly by Mr. Tindall, the rural mail carrier.

Skeeter Williams stuck his head in the door briefly, nodded at Mr. Rush, but walked on toward Livingston's when he saw the number that had already gathered. Skeeter's appearance, personality, and talent made him stand out among the characters who came to town on Saturdays.

After the usual round of greetings as each new customer

filed in came an uneasy quiet after their eyes noticed Henny and the PW across his chest. A few nodded to him but said nothing.

Mr. Sif's middle son, Alec, appeared in the doorway fully dressed in his army greens. An explosion of greetings followed, with Mrs. Freeman hugging Alec and the men shaking his hand and patting him on the back.

"Our boys are really lickin' 'em now," Mr. Franklin announced, holding up the headlines in the *Times and Democrat*. "Them Natzis and Japs are backing up so fast they ain't got much room left to back."

Jake Hutto glided past the open door, making a coarse "ribit, ribit" in passing.

"Ribit, ribit," echoed from the direction of the twins.

"Now which one of you done that?" Mrs. Freeman was in front of the twins, quizzing two expressionless faces.

Fatneck was unperturbed, his clippers gnawing without falter around my right ear. I concealed my enjoyment of the mockery and the innocence in the twin's faces, holding back all but a limited smile.

"That'll be ten cents, Will," Mr. Rush said as he lowered the chair. He paused momentarily and whisked the white hair from the chair seat before asking, "Who's next?"

"Do you want yours cut?" I asked in Henny's direction.

"Now, James," Mr. Franklin began in a rarely heard salutation to Fatneck, "you ain't gonna cut no Natzi's hair when we got a U-S American soldier waiting here in uniform, is ya?"

"But we were here fir—" I started, in an attempt to insist on the priority our early arrival should have secured.

Everyone had come to their feet as they felt the confrontation grow.

"Now, everybody, jes' settle down," Fatneck growled, trying to calm the situation. His face was thoroughly reddened and the tumor bulged above his collar. "I ain't cuttin' no Natzi hair in heah anytime. Not now. Not anytime! Will, you just git on along. And you take your Natzi man with you. We don't want no trouble in heah," he added in a quieter voice.

"But, Mr. Rush—" I protested as Henny pulled me toward the door.

"Come, Vill. Ve cannot be trouble, here. Haircut, nein, I do not want haircut. Nein," he cautioned.

"It just ain't fair!" I yelled in final protest. I continued in a more deliberate tone to Jake, who had returned to the doorside, "Ole Fatneck, he don't half know how to cut hair, nohow."

Barbershops were ubiquitous in small Southern towns. Neeses was but one in a series of towns strewn along the railroad from Columbia to Augusta. Each served as the hub for the surrounding miles of farmland, providing for a hundred or so farms a source of general supplies, a cotton gin, and churches. Neeses terminated a sequence of names taken by towns to the west, Norway, Denmark, and Sweden. Other than the names, there was little to distinguish one from another. The residents knew no reason the towns were so named and laid no claim to Scandinavian heritage. And although an engraving on an aging tombstone in the local cemetery identified John Neece as the founding father of Neeses, it was a fact known by very few.

\* \* \*

The Methodists and Baptists of Neeses held forth from opposite ends of town. While serving as the forum for delivery of the Word to a general admixture of whites, the churches served broader civic functions. They provided the best method for dispersing community gossip, the means for organizing charity for any who had fallen on hard times, and the base for all community endeavors. The two churches came together whenever circumstances required it; and they celebrated the harvest, abundant or meager, together, forming the poles around which the fall baseball game was organized. They argued little over theology, most folks identifying with one church or the other because of family tradition. The colored churches located away from town took more pastoral settings and, to me, lengthy and mysterious names, but they served similar functions for the sharecroppers.

No other congregating places cut across the whole society as did the churches, but others existed, to be sure. The icehouse was one. This small, thick-walled vault located next to the coal yard held the town's supply of ice, trucked in every Thursday from a production center in Orangeburg. A jug of corn liquor was always available there. Among other commodities, the icehouse also secured the town's only supply of rubbers. Placed along the ledge over the entrance, the range of supplies dispensed by the icehouse was known to all boys in Neeses for years before any serious need for the products would arise. Just being seen hanging around the icehouse enhanced the notoriety of teens in search of their maturity. Control of the rubbers gave iceman John Paul Whittle current knowledge of who was sleeping with whom and made his out-of-the-way establishment a favorite, frequented by young men in search of this information.

Colored and whites alike also congregated on the covered walkway in the front of Livingston's Mercantile. A few of the older men whittled away at walking sticks, whistles, and chinaberry popguns. But most just stood around, exchanging small talk and tapping their feet to the music.

Inside, the music was more intense, originating about halfway back near the potbellied stove. No one noticed as Henny and I eased in past the penny candy case to the left of the front door. The beat of the music could be felt throughout the store in the pine plank floor, now sagging away from the sills and stringers from years of bearing plow shares, hog feed, and benches piled high with rolls of cloth and various hardware.

Several men were gathered around Jme, completely absorbed in making intricate contributions from their instruments. On Saturdays the music was nearly continuous from late morning until dark, with only a break at noon time to listen to "Snuffy Jenkins and the Hired Hands" on radio station WIS.

Jme's lifelong love for music had intensified after his accident. He now had more time to devote to playing, and on weekdays when most other men were busy on the farms, he dabbled a bit at composing, mostly gospel songs. Skeeter Williams was one of the few others with time during the week to play.

Skeeter was about twenty-one, and next to Jme was considered the best musician in the area. So far as the United States, or South Carolina, or even Orangeburg county was concerned, Skeeter didn't exist. He was born at home and his birth was never registered. He didn't specifically dodge the draft, as the local gossip would have it, he just never appeared on the county's draft roster. Locally no one felt he would have made much difference in the war, anyway. He stood barely five-feet tall, and nowhere had nature gone farther awry than in Skeeter's face. His small head, with eyes so small they barely made any openings at all, was perched atop a lean and dwarfed frame. His facial tissues were so frail that they left only a hollow where cheekbones should be and made vague undulations in the skin over the upper teeth.

He was good at his music, but not much else. At least, not as far as most people knew. He could catch a fish too and spent much of his time along the South Edisto, pole-fishing for redbreast bream, setting out line for river cats, and dynamiting the deep-running mudfish. And he always knew how to find bootleg whiskey.

Skeeter drove a shiny Ford coupe, a sure sign to Granny Jack that he knew more about bootleg whiskey than just where to find it. Granny Jack was also suspicious of Jme in this regard. He owned one of the two stores in town with access to the amount of sugar needed for a still.

And he liked a little nip of "white" on Saturday while playing with the boys.

Skeeter could fill in with any instrument, although the "hound dog" dobro was his favorite. Jme had taught him virtually everything he knew about music, and the two relished each other's company no matter what the occasion.

Today Skeeter and Jme were accompanied by Artie Tindall—whose three-finger banjo picking added sparkle to every song—and Sam Corbet, whose monotonous bass was lost in the drumming of shoes on the plank floor.

Leopold Jamison sat outside the circle on a couple sacks of

meal. He was the only Negro the group ever accepted. When he wasn't busy carrying out groceries or supplies for someone, his choppy harmonica danced about the surface of the others' music. Leo had been with Jme and Minnie off and on since their marriage, working as Jme's valet and doing any heavy work required in the store.

* * *

"That just embarrasses me," Minnie was telling Granny Jack. "You, my own kin, counting change after me. It looks like you don't trust me. Or that I can't count."

"Minnie, I'm sorry it embarrasses you, but I always count my change. There ain't nobody that's perfect, not even you."

"Well, you don't have to be obvious about it. Not with all these other folks in heah."

Granny Jack smiled only slightly as she tucked the change and ration stamps inside her purse, snapped it shut, and started packing her purchases in an Octagon soap box.

Jme's group was now breaking down on "Fancy Gap," the most popular of a few of his compositions, which had caught on with stage performers elsewhere in the state. It had a lightening pace and opportunity for each instrument to shine, ingredients necessary for longstanding success for music of this type.

The brass tip on Uncle Jme's peg was used to keep time with the music. The brass was flattened and burred at the edges from years of hobbling about on the bricked streets of Neeses. The marks of his comings and goings were stamped on almost every wooden floor in town. He kept the devilish schoolboy glint in his eyes, little suppressed by the extra folds of skin across his eyelids. The late addition of a goatee had enhanced the mystique that surrounded him.

In all, he seemed a bit out of place as a storekeeper, but then Minnie and Leo carried out all the obligations of proprietorship. A few appropriately spaced stamps with Jme's peg were sufficient to gain attention to any task he wanted accomplished.

"Fancy Gap" ended abruptly with a chromatic run from Artie's banjo. Henny nodded a greeting to the five but made no attempt to speak. Jme hadn't adjusted to the presence of Henny and the other POWs on his brother's farm but did not make an issue of his displeasure. After all, he was among the state representatives who had pressed the War Department to make the POWs available for farm labor.

The music had almost made me forget to relate the barber shop incident to Granny Jack. "Heah's a nickel back. He only charged me a dime," I reported. "Henny didn't get his cut. Ole Fatneck wouldn't cut it just because Alec Tyler came in then with his uniform on."

"Now, mind yo' mouth, Will," Granny Jack corrected.

"I ain't kidding. He wouldn't cut it," I repeated.

"Well, we'll see about that," she promised, motioning for me to pick up the box she had packed.

"No Miss Jack, I do not want to have haircut. I will have at camp."

As we left Uncle Jme's store, the ACL local from Augusta to Columbia was puffing into town. On Saturday mornings the train always stopped while the crew took their lunch, whether or not passengers or freight were to be loaded or unloaded. Black smoke belching from the locomotive, hissing of air valves from below, and the screeching of metal on metal filled the town. Any haul with over six cars severed the main street into two corridors and completely blocked cross traffic in the two-block long town.

Jessie Waymeyer was a corpulent colored woman who seemed to spend most of her time in town. Her obesity was exceeded only by her meanness. She had only one child, Jervey, now five years old. The colored people were no less embarrassed by Jessie than whites. Probably most annoying was her management of Jervey while in town. Jervey was a backwards child who was easily thrown into hysterics by loud noises. Neeses was perhaps a good place for him during the weekdays, when things were quiet. On Saturdays, however, the noises generated in even the small town constantly assaulted his calm. Perhaps worst of all was the train. At the first sound of a train, Jessie took a direct approach in her efforts to overcome his panic: she would hold him as close to the track as possible as the train pulled through town—Jervey screaming and trying to get away all the time.

The sight of the frantic Jervey trying to escape his mother's grasp—alternately clutching at her ears, clawing, and kicking—immobilized Henny. He fixed on the scene momentarily, then proceeded, visibly against his will, to climb onto the wagon.

"Jessie, you oughta be ashamed o' yo'self, treatin' dis chile dis away," Leo's wife was admonishing.

"You black cracker. You ain't got no say heah," Jessie retorted.

"Maybe I ain't got no say. But you got it coming if someone took a stick and laid you out."

"Yeah, you talk on, ole lady. You better get back in de sto' with yo' white cracker friends, 'fo I lay you out."

Alec arrived at the entrance to Livingston's as Granny Jack was maneuvering herself into the back of the wagon. His utterance to the other men there about "Natzi's being all over town" was loud enough for Henny's and my benefit but apparently passed Granny Jacks aging acuity.

When evening came, Granny Jack prepared for her foot washing routine in the back hallway.

"Oh, Will, I almost forgot," she said, "I must give you something."

"What's that, Granny?" I asked.

"I want you to take this money and put it aside for church tomorrow." She handed me two dollars and twenty cents.

"What is all this money for?" I asked, astonished at the amount, more than ten times the amount I had ever taken to church before.

"Just count it penitence from Minnie and me. I guess if I can forgive her arrogance, the good Lord will forgive me for taking her money for a little while."

# CHAPTER NINE

The *Times and Democrat*.. "Eisenhower's Tornado Of Fire Stunning. Germans Attacked From Front and Rear. Hold On Normandy Steadily Expanded By Anglo-Saxons." June 7, 1944.

Supreme Headquarters, Allied Expeditionary Force, Wednesday, June 7 (AP)—United States, British and Canadian troops battled inland against Nazi defenses of Normandy across the white-capped English Channel today to expand an invasion operation which Prime Minister Churchill said was proceeding "in a thoroughly satisfactory manner" and with unexpectedly light casualties.

Channel weather was adverse, a strong northeaster kicking up the waves. But this was not permitted to halt the stream of reinforcements and supplies for the forces hacking out positions along a 100-mile front between Cherbourg and LeHarve.

The German radio expressed fear of further landings. Fresh and strong naval forces were reportedly sighted this morning off the Dunkerque-Calais area, opposite Dover and some 200 miles airline northeast of Cherbourg.

The Nazi-controlled Paris radio said "an important American-British naval squadron was cruising off Cherbourg two hours after midnight."

Gen. Dwight D. Eisenhower, supreme commander, was serene and confident of success in the great land, sea and air blow, launched before dawn Tuesday under a screen of bombs and shells from 4,000 warships and 11,000 warplanes.

\* \* \*

Even at one o'clock in the morning, the day's heat had not dissipated. The periodic clicking of the telegraph could be heard through the depot window, open for the station master to gain any night air that might stir. Colored men, mostly old, stood in several masses in the station yard and on the platform, wiping perspiration from their foreheads and arms as they talked. Younger children raced about under the platform, across the tracks and around the horses and wagons tied up in the periphery. Only a few women remained, mostly gathered around Doni, admiring the sleeping month-old infant cradled against her breast.

Many folks had been there all afternoon, having come directly from Sunday services at Macedonia Church. Others had come and gone throughout the day, bringing food and lingering in conversation for a while. The crowd had thinned out when Melvin didn't arrive on the five o'clock run. A couple white men, Uncle Jme and Skeeter Williams in their number, clumped together next to the station house.

Granny Jack never remained in town after dark, and she had left by midafternoon for the walk back to the farmplace. Aunt Minnie had intervened on my behalf by initially proposing that I sleep at their house, but eventually assuring that I would be on the wagon home with Champ's family.

After the five o'clock train passed through without stopping, I dallied about the depot, mostly to be with Sugarbread. As darkness came, any thought of my walking home alone diminished. Even without the cemetery at the crest of Tyler's hill, I could not do it. The cemetery entirely precluded any passage.

Rarely did I have the chance to remain in Neeses at night.

Once or twice a year, gypsies would pass through town and throw up a fair for a two- or three-night stand. Granny Jack had relented on several occasions over the years, giving me a few cents "to throw away," forbidding entrance into any of the tents, and requiring that I spend the night with Uncle Jme and Aunt Minnie.

Once, I had been allowed to witness the celebration that surrounded the arrival of Uncle Jme's new wooden leg. It, too, had arrived on the night train. It seemed as if the entire town turned out then. Men had ambled back and forth between the platform and the wagon and pickups, where gallons of "white" passed among them. Young and old alike had danced on the platform to the music of Jme and his friends.

The anticipation had peaked with the lowering of a crate stamped on all sides "MFD in Manchester" from a boxcar. Jme broke open the crate and thrust above his head a shiny brass-tipped leg. He'd immediately strapped it to his thigh stump and danced with every willing woman and quite a few men.

Tonight was different. The air felt cool. The crowd was quiet. All of us anticipated the Southbound eight o'clock train from Columiba.

"It's coming up de tracks now, Daddy," Sugarbread called out.

"Get back away from dose tracks, you chilluns," Champ ordered.

"Lawd, those chilluns do worry me so 'round dese tracks," added a colored voice next to Doni.

As the train pulled alongside the station, with its main beam searching back and forth, a wail went up from the crowd and tears flowed from nearly every eye. New outcries burst forth as the boxcar door opened and the flag-draped casket bearing Melvin's body was pushed onto the platform. The wooden casket was lifted onto a wagon by Champ and three other men. The slow lantern-lit cortege headed into the countryside.

When we arrived at the churchyard the next day with Mr. Sif, wagons were pulled under all of the surrounding trees; mules were tied to tree trunks and the sides of other wagons. The PW truck was parked at the roadside, and Henny, Enno, and the driver stood with hands folded. All of the pews at Macedonia Church filled with murmuring, sobbing Negroes. Reverend Phillips met us at the door and led us through a sea of black, tear-stained faces to the front, where he motioned for us to sit on the pew with Champ and his family. Melvin's casket rested on sawhorses at the head of the middle aisle, open, with the wooden top on the floor propped against the horse legs.

Church rarely held much of an attraction for me. Granny Jack saw to it that I went to church with the Baptists every Sunday that the weather permitted. I prayed for rain.

When Mr. Sif visited the Baptists was the exception. Mr. Sif was a Methodist, an elder in his church, but found reason to join the Baptists several times a year. Among the Baptists he was held with the same respect as the deacons and was always invited down to sit with their number in a group of short pews to the right of the pulpit. This small section was adjacent to Clara and Sarah's corner. The twins had total charge of the church's music. Clara played a loud and steady piano and Sara filled the gaps with the sweet flow of the violin. Both had taken turns at marriage to Fatneck Rush, but they now lived alone, together, within view of the church, in a wide-porched house with a hexagonal gable on the morning end.

Mr. Sif's presence further enlivened the spirited Baptist meetings. He privately maintained that Methodists didn't know how to sing and were constrained by songs with little rhythm and a confusion of words only understandable to the Wesleys. Baptist voices strained to keep pace and volume with Mr. Sif. From any place in the room—his voice peaked above the others, and at verses' end lingered well beyond the others' last note. Clara spiked the hymns with extra runs, filling every available interval and backing Mr. Sif's terminal drone. Sara's violin was lost in the musical conflagration except to those in the first few rows.

Preacher Lewis usually obliged by adding a few extra hymns. "That sounded so good, why don't we turn to page eighty-seven and sing all verses of 'Shall We Gather at the River.'" Such additions necessitated that the preaching be cut short, a consequence receiving near unanimous approval.

Reverend Phillips had come by the farm on the previous day to ask Granny Jack to say a few words at Melvin's service. She had declined, promising to get Mr. Sif to speak in her place.

Reverend Phillips greeted the gathering and led them in prayer, thanking the Lord for an extended list of items. The prayer covered some period of time, with few things moving or fixed on the earth escaping specific citation. "Amens" and "It's de truth" punctuated most every phrase and came in a chorus as he exhausted his inventory.

"We thank Miz Jack and Mastuh Will and Mistuh Tyla . . ." Reverend Phillips started.

"Yes, we do!" echoed from several voices scattered in the background.

"We thank them for coming heah on dis sad day . . ." he continued, and paused for a new round of affirmations from his fold. "We'd be honored if dey care to say any words over dis our deceased brother."

Mr. Sif pushed out into the aisle and accepted Reverend Phillips' assistance onto the platform behind the casket. He paused and looked around the congregation, nodding as he made contact with coloreds that he knew, which were most. His cane slipped from his left hand, rattling against the wooden planks before Reverend Phillips could retrieve it. After finding a secure place for the cane across the pulpit, he hesitated for a moment, looking out over the hushed assembly, then down into the open casket, and finally directly at the occupants of the first pew. Mr. Sif began in a somber tone.

"My dear friends," he started, "we come heah to share the loss of this boy with our brother and sister, Champ and Doni. This . . ." he continued, the sweat already trickling down his face, "is a day to celebrate! Cause this boy's now on the right hand o'God."

"Sho it's the truth," came a voice from the rear. The congregation seemed to be with him from the first word, and every pause called forth a salvo of encouragement.

"I got boys, and Mrs. Jack, she's got boys, and lots of you got yo' own boys, suffering right now on them foreign shores. But Melvin, he ain't suffering no more," Mr. Sif continued.

"Some of them boys are worried 'bout us back heah. But Melvin, he can look down and see that Champ and Doni and these children are all okay. He even knows that Cephas is heah, just as calm as he can be."

"Hallelujah, he sees us all."

"Praise the Lawd. Keep on looking down, Melvin."

A broad smile broke across Cephas' face as he chanted, "Thank you, Lawd. Thank you, Lawd."

"Some of them boys are wounded, and some lie in trenches, scared fo' their lives."

"They ain't no feah in de Land o'Jordan."

Looking again into the casket, Mr. Sif pointed to the still body. "Melvin's flesh ain't torn, and he ain't scared."

"He ain't got no feah."

"Ain't no mis'ry."

"And some of us right here on this land, we suffer along today. We get too much rain or we get no rain a'tall. We get the boweevil in the cotton and we get the cutworm in our corn. But Melvin, he don't suffer with these miseries. He gets just the light sprinkle each day and his cotton and corn ain't burned by the summer sun."

"Say it, Lawd, ain't it the truth!"

"Hallelujah!"

"He ain't suffering now."

"And some of us here, we're done bent over with author-itis and our light grows dim. But Melvin, he don't need no cane and he don't need no spectacles."

"He don't need no cane," they chanted as Mr. Sif raised his cane and spectacles over his head.

"Yea, Lawd he do see clear."

"Tell it now."

"All he hears is the angel's music as he feasts on everything he wants from God's bounty, waitin' on the day he's gonna be united with his loved ones. He is gonna be in that chariot when it swoops down to get Champ. . . ."

"Hallelujah, wont they be some joy."

". . . and when it swoops down to get Doni. . . ."

"Yes, he will."

"He'll be driving that chariot."

"Glory, glory, he'll be drivin'. . . ."

"And when it swoops down to get his brothers and sisters—"

"Yeah, Lawd, where's Melvin gonna be?"

"—he is gonna ride right by their side," Mr. Sif concluded.

"Let 'im ride."

The piano hit a couple of notes, but for the moment, Mr. Sif prevailed.

"And Melvin, well he's looking down right now from glory and he is looking for a smile from his friends and a smile from his family 'cause they know how happy he is. And a song on our lips, praising the Lord."

This time the piano couldn't be held off. With a few strong chords, the clapping and chanting was brought into synchrony, and Reverend Phillips was on his feet leading out with "I Look Over Jordan."

After a few bars into the first verse, Reverend Phillips let the music carry on its own, shook Mr. Sif's hand, and helped him down from the pulpit and back to his place alongside Granny Jack.

Crepe myrtle draped the casket and hung from each open window, its pale fragrance overwhelmed by the odors of bodies and hair dressings. The sprawling live oaks provided sufficient shade to keep the occupants of the small church from boiling.

Mr. Sif had hardly reached a pew before the chanting, clapping mourners spilled into the aisles, and migrated toward the casket.

Bertha Porterfield always sat close behind a grieving family in circumstances like this. In addition to her steady volleys of encouragement to the preacher, she always wanted to be available to console the family. She also could always be counted upon to fall out if the pitch of emotion threatened to abate prematurely. Bertha knew just how to pick her moment and to fall with arms flung overhead, body twirling, a climactic scream, and a fall backwards into the arms of a catcher. Her generous breasts provided a substantial stop, preventing her from sliding through the catcher's grasp. A rather steady parade of sisters fell out in the usual course of events, so Bertha's participation was not required often. But she remained always prepared.

Although most of the Black men had robust muscles from their years of hard labor, the catcher's job, when such occasions arose, required strength and timing. They not only needed to support and to carry the worshipper who fell out to a pew, they had to know when and where to grab. One miscalculation could lead to a wailing member on the floor, or alternatively a premature grab around the bust of a sister who had no intention of falling out that day. Hot weather and perspiration made the situation worse, demanding a cool head, good timing, and a bit of a sense of distraction from the proceedings.

Melvin's casket top was nailed down, the congregation crying out anew as each blow of the hammer reverberated through the small church. Four Negroes lifted the casket to their shoulders, carried it down the aisle, and out to the waiting wagon. The mules were led some two hundred yards through the woods to a clearing where a grave had been dug next to the remains of a younger brother who had died in infancy. The congregation marched along behind, led by the family, the white contingent, and the Reverend Phillips. All joined in chanting the strains of "Just a Closer Walk With Thee." Doni fell across the casket with convulsing sobs after the flag had been folded by Mr. Sif and Reverend Phillips.

The crowd began to disperse, some lingering in groups around the other grave sites as clumps of sandy soil were shoveled over the casket. Champ had carved a small cross, which he pushed into the soft mound when it was done.

Champ thanked Mr. Sif for his words over Melvin, and Granny Jack for coming. As he passed in front of Henny and Enno, he spat on the ground and walked on.

# CHAPTER TEN

The *Times and Democrat*, Friday, June 16. "Yanks Strike At Nipponese In Homeland"

Washington, June 15— (AP)—America's new super Fortress bombed Japan's homeland today and the Tokyo radio, acknowledging attacks, said industrial areas of Moji and Shimonoseki were hit. . . .

An imperial Japanese communique estimated the number of raiding planes at 20 and made the usual claims that they were "intercepted and repulsed." It said several were shot down and Domei, Japanese news agency, said six were shot down.

The Japanese said both B-29 super Fortresses and B-24 Liberators were among the American planes. . . .

The War Department disclosed at 1:30 p.m., Eastern War Time, that the long-secret flying giants had gone into action. The announcement said:

"B-29 super Fortresses of the United States Army Air Forces 20th Bomber Command bombed Japan today."

To this was added some time later that the planes flew to the attack from the China-India-Burma theater. . . .

It was the second American bombing of Japan, but

the first announcement of action by the B-29s. . . .

"It is now officially confirmed that American super Fortresses flying from remote bases have successfully bombed Tokyo in a very heavy raid," Starnes told the house.

"It can be safely assumed that these were the new B-29s.

"It may be safely assumed that these planes approached Tokyo at an altitude of more than 30,000 feet and a speed of more than 300 miles per hour with the heaviest bomb loads and the greatest armaments of any airplanes in the world.

"This is a new day in warfare, and it will hasten the end of the war. . . ."

Secretary of War Stimson said the bombings represented the beginning of another phase of the war in the Pacific, and declared that no corner of the Japanese homeland is now safe from attack. . . .

By hitting the Japanese war industries again and again and again, the great planes may change the whole complexion of the Pacific conflict and hasten the day of Japan's utter defeat.

\* \* \*

Enemies intent on the destruction of the farmers' livelihoods attacked during the hottest month. At times, the weather could take a substantial toll. Entire fields of waist-high corn could shrivel and never recover from a drought of three weeks. An untimely hailstorm could beat a crop at any stage of maturity into the dirt. Farmers took these disasters in stride, knowing that the weather was also their greatest asset. Various pests that silently worked the fields were another matter—the boll weevil being most notorious.

This small perennial nemesis first gained a foothold in Texas, and from that base crept northward and eastward until all of the cotton producing land was within its domain. Over the years, cotton planters had adopted various strategies to outmaneuver the insidious insect. They planted earlier and earlier in an attempt to get the cotton bolls fixed before hot weather arrived and weevils wielded their greatest destruction. By the forties, most farmers had come to rely on "sweet poison"—generally molasses and calcium arsenate—as their most effective weapon.

Each year molasses was put up in gallon cans and stored in the shed against Champ's barn. A few cans were consumed during the winter months, but most remained in readiness for counterattacks once signs of the weevil invasion were spotted.

The first two sweeps through the thirty-eight acres of cotton had proceeded smoothly this year. Henny and the other POWs worked steadily alongside Champ, Cephas, Sugarbread, and me. Doni remained at the wagon readying fresh buckets of the poison. One pound of arsenic stirred into a gallon each of water and molasses gave up a sufficient amount of the mixture to mop an acre of cotton plants.

"Make sho' ta hit all de top leaves and de squares," Champ instructed repeatedly, in an effort to secure the most effective application. "It don't do no good on de groun'."

Champ had noted the emergence of red spiders and cotton lice in substantial numbers after mopping with molasses and arsenic and tried to suppress these opportunists by adding sulfur and nicotine to the mopping mixture.

Granny Jack worried about having the POWs back on the farm so soon after Melvin's burial but knew that Champ's crew alone couldn't handle the poison application. She was finding more and more squares that had been bored by the weevil and fallen from the plants and recognized she couldn't delay any longer. She planned for the POWs to arrive on Thursday and finish the mopping by noon on Saturday.

Her presence in the fields, Granny Jack had told me, would decrease the likelihood of any confrontation. She and Wilhelm shared the mixing job at the wagon, the three other POWs went in one direction, Champ's family and me in the opposite.

Completion of the mopping just after noon on Saturday brought surprises that removed any final tension—if any, in fact, had existed. The first of which was Henny pulling from his lunch sack a stitched Spaulding baseball and tossing it to me.

"It's for you and Sugarbread."

"Wow!" I exclaimed, tossing it up several times and then over to Sugarbread. The annual Harvest Game was the only time I had held a leather covered baseball. "How'd you git it?"

"It was in the storeroom and no one used it at all. I gave a bronze cross for it. Ve may be able to trade for the—what you say?" He demonstrated pounding one fist into the other.

"A glove?"

"Ja, the glove. I think there are five or six there."

"Will you try to get one?"

"Ja, if I can. But I do not have any more medals."

"Thank you, Henny." I hugged him quickly, and Sugarbread and I separated to try out the priceless acquisition. Henny smiled and relaxed against a chinaberry tree, watching us as he pulled a sandwich from the paper sack.

Champ appeared at his front door holding two pies piled high with meringue. He handed one to Granny Jack, who was resting on the porch steps before walking home. He approached Wilhelm with the second pie.

"My Doni made this pie for y'all men," Champ said, extending it to Wilhelm.

"What is?" Wilhelm questioned.

"Lemon meringue," Granny Jack interjected. "Doni makes 'em better'n anyone around."

"Ve will have it at the camp tonight. Thank you," Wilhelm said, holding it up for all the men to see.

On the return from Champ's house, as we neared the crest of the hill beyond our swimming hole, Granny Jack asked, "I saw on the way to the spring some piles of dirt. Y'all been digging in the woods?"

"Yes m'am, Sugarbread and me."

"What on earth are y'all doing?"

"We're just looking for arrowheads," I explained.

Indeed, during lulls between the waves of molasses and arsenic applications, Sugarbread and I had worked episodically at the mound. When we uncovered the first bone, we realized how close we were to Indian treasures. We carefully covered the hole with a mat woven of pine saplings and straw when we left the gravesite. Our last dig had taken us halfway up a body and almost to one foot. We could tell now that the first bone we had encountered was a rib.

Daily, we had enlarged the hole to the point that we were completely enclosed in an excavated cave. Not knowing which direction would reveal the treasures buried with our Indian, we gradually dug in all directions, carefully breaking every clump of earth to prevent discarding precious artifacts.

"You had better confine your arrowhead hunting to what you can find in the fields and git those holes filled back in. One of the animals will break a leg stepping in those holes," Granny Jack told me.

"Yes m'am. I promise. Will you put the ball on the mantle for me?" I asked.

"That was a nice present. Did you thank Henny?"

"Yes M'am."

"Where're y'all going now?"

"We're gonna check our rabbit boxes befo' coming home."

"Thanks again for the baseball," I called to Henny as he and Granny Jack and the other men walked on to the house to meet the PW truck.

When Sugarbread and I returned to the mound, we saw the mat was disturbed, twisted half in and half out, with one edge of it perceptibly moving. Sugarbread refused to go any closer.

"The dead done come back."

"Oh, Sugarbread, you don't believe that. There is just some animal that's fell through. Come on and let's check it."

"Nooooo suh. I ain't going nowheah near dat grave."

"Come on, Sugarbread. If that's one of Granny's pigs, she will skin us alive."

"If it's one of them Injuns, he'll take the skin of'n our heads. I ain't going nowheah near dat grave."

"Will you stay heah, if I check it?"

"I ain't going no inch closer'n I am. You can do what you want."

I edged slowly toward the hole, trying to keep one eye on Sugarbread and one eye on the mat, which was now quivering constantly. One major jerk of the mat sent me running back toward Sugarbread, now about twice the distance away from where we'd started.

"Let's look in from a tree," I suggested, reckoning that to be safer.

"Come on, Will, let's get out of heah."

"We can't leave, Granny Jack's done warned us."

"I ain't never going close to dat grave. You must be crazy!"

Sugarbread helped me onto the first limb of a large persimmon tree and I shinnied up to get a look into the grave.

"What you see, Will?"

"I can't see nothing yet. I gotta go a little higher."

"What color's a Injun?" I asked Sugarbread, spotting something in the hole.

"Dey's red, you know dat."

"Do you reckon they turn black when they go to heaven?"

"What you talking 'bout? What's going on?"

"There is a black Injun in that grave, thrashing all about." With that, Sugarbread shimmied up the tree beside me.

"That ain't no colored Injun," Sugarbread corrected, "dat be Cephas. I kin see his red shirt."

"Now Champ is gonna skin us, too," I said. "We better git down from here and get Cephas out of the grave."

The job was impossible, even when he was still, we couldn't pull him out. Every time he jerked, it frightened us, causing our grip to loosen and Cephas to slide back to the bottom with the bones.

"There ain't no use. We can't get him out. Let's go get Champ."

"Daddy will kill bof'us if he know what we been up to."

"Well, we got to do something, we can't just let him lay in there with all those bones."

"Let's find Mr. Henny. He'll hep us."

We both raced up to the house to get Henny, who was helping

Granny Jack nail some wire around the bottom of the pigpen.

"Henny, come help us. We need your help down at the spring."

"Hold on, you kids. Can't you see Henny's busy here."

"It's Cephas. He's had a fit," I stated.

"And he done crawl in the hole with the bones."

"He's what?"

"He done fall in the hole with the bones and we can't git him out."

"Henny, you'd better go see what you can do. I think I need to know some more about what you kids are up to," forewarned Granny Jack as we departed.

Henny pushed Cephas out of the hole in the side of the mound and then crawled out himself, leaving loose bones scrambled in the bottom.

"How long has he been here, Vill?"

"We don't know. We just found him here and came running for help."

"Well, ve have to get him home. Does he have any medicine for his fit?"

"He got some, but he ain't been taking none since he seed Mr. Wartman de last time," Sugarbread answered.

Henny lifted the frail frame onto his arms and started through the woods toward the tenant house.

"Sugarbread, you run and find Champ and tell him ve're coming."

Henny was in the cornfield beyond the woods before we met Champ. Henny was drenched—his feet and britches' legs from crossing the creek, and the rest from the sweat that was streaming down his cheeks.

"He stopped jerking about half vay here," Henny announced to Champ.

"I'll take my boy, Mr. Henny."

"Do you have some medicine you can give him?"

"He is aw'right now. We will take care of him."

Champ took the limp body in his arms, walked to end of a row of corn, and turned in the direction of home.

Perhaps it would never happen. Still, I wished to see Champ and Henny in lockstep, tending to some farm chore. Any shared farm chore might engage their skills and fill in the gulf between them.

After the POWs left and the skies darkened, I knew the time for Granny Jack's footwashing was approaching and, as I anticipated, this time it would involve more than footwashing.

"Tell me about you and Sugarbread digging in the mound." Granny Jack started.

"We were just looking for treasures, tomahawks, arrows and other things that were buried with the Indians in the mound." I explained.

"Who told you Indians were buried in the mound?" Granny Jack countered.

"Nobody, I guess, maybe Champ mentioned it." I answered.

"Champ knows better. He was probably just trying to keep you away from it. That mound was made to bury several calves that died one Spring. For several years, Champ added to the mound to keep the burial safe."

"But Sugarbread and I . . ." I tried to interject.

"We don't know what killed the calves that Spring, but you could have caught some disease digging around with their bones," Granny Jack stated. "But more important, if it had been an Indian grave, you have no business disturbing it, for tomahawks, arrowheads or anything else."

I can't remember if any footwashing was done that evening, but I remember well the sacredness of burial grounds, Indians or anyone else. I have even come to believe that the same applies to the burial places of animals.

# CHAPTER ELEVEN

The *Times and Democrat.* "Nazi Officers Held Prisoner Voice Optimism," *Times and Democrat,* June 19, 1944.

With British Forces in France, June 18—(AP, by Roger D. Greene)—Captured German officers said today they still expected Germany to win the war and they pinned their faith on the robot bomber as "our great weapon of the war."

"Soon we will destroy London and other big cities of England with our pilotless planes," boasted a 46-year-old Colonel.

"We have enough of these planes to destroy the Isle of Wight in four hours. Your night fighters cannot stop them. Nothing can stop them. That's why we're going to win the war."

In the next breath the Colonel acknowledged:

"It is worse for us in this war than in the last because we have too many fronts."

Like all German officers taken prisoner, the Colonel began to spout a machine-gun stream of words when asked if the Fuehrer still is popular in Germany despite defeats on the Russian and Italian fronts. When they start on "Mein Fuehrer" they talk like automatons. You can see it has been drilled into them. As officers they say the "correct" things. But German privates spat at the name "Hitler. . . ."

Two things German prisoners fear: First, being turned over to the Russian prisoners they have forced to fight on their side; second, being sent to Siberia.

They neither understand nor appreciate human decency of the Allies. One prisoner, told to dig a slit trench as a protection against air raids and shelling, wept like a baby. He thought he was digging his own grave.

* * *

Sheriff Boggs had come to the farm on several occasions, most recently when he was running for re-election. He wanted Granny Jack's vote and offered her one dollar for each of her Negroes she could get to vote for him.

"Otis," she had told him, "you know I will vote for you. But as for my farm hands, they ain't never voted and if they did, I wouldn't tell them who to vote for."

The long hood of the sheriff's black Buick was studded with gleaming chrome and embellished with a flying goddess that jutted forward over its vertical grill. The engine's powerful grind idled for a moment and then shut down. Sugarbread and I walked around the spectacular machine, studying and touching every detail. We knew every car owned in town and searched the *Times and Democrat* for pictures of others. Farmers invariably owned Model As or Chevrolets. The Watkin's man also sold wares from a Model A crowded to the roof with tiny bottles and boxes. Mr. Tindall delivered mail in a green Studebaker Champion, the only car in Neeses that violated Henry Ford's dictum, "You can have any color you desire, so long as it's black."

"Mawnin' Miz Jack," Sheriff Boggs greeted in a soft voice.

"Mawnin' Otis. You're out'n around right early this mawnin.'"

"Yo' place sho' looks nice, Miz Jack. How's yo' cotton crop?"

"I think we got a good stand, if we can keep down the bo' weevil. Just started mopping the squares a couple weeks ago."

"You git a good 'lotment this yeah?"

"About thirty-eight acres, same as last year."

"I hope it makes good fer ya."

"Thank you, Otis, it looks good so far."

"I saw down the road yo' ditches need cuttin' back. I'm gonna send out the chain gang in the next few weeks to clean 'em up fer ya."

"I 'preciate it. They are grow'd over a good bit."

Prince growled and barked a few times before settling down at the end of his chain. One of Sugarbread's hounds inspected the Buick with us, hiked his leg, and sprayed one of the front white walls.

"Miz Jack, I'm gonna hafta take Champ in."

"Whaddaya mean, Otis. He ain't been nowhere but heah."

"They's been a problem at Norway Camp. Looks like a bunch of them Kraut's been poisoned. Two of 'em's dead and don't know if another one's gonna make it.

"How you know they been poisoned?"

"We don't know for sho, but ole Doc Connor says it looks awfly suspicious. The sick ones got to retching and wound up hemmergin' from both ends."

"Is Henny okay?" I interrupted.

"I can't keep 'em all straight. Jus' know that two and maybe three of 'em by now's dead."

"That's just awful, Otis, but what's it all got to do with Champ?" Granny Jack asked.

"Looks like all the sick ones been out heah. Say they all had some of a pie Champ had give 'em."

"Ain't nothing wrong with the pies. Doni cooked 'em right here in my house. We had a piece last night."

"Well, like I say, it looks awfly suspicious at this point. We got some tests going up to Fort Jackson."

"I'll vouch for Champ if you leave him heah til this gets straightened out."

"Think in the situation we got heah, involvin' those Krauts and Champ just buryin' his boy and all, I better take 'im in."

"Lemme git my hat and I'll go 'round to the place with you."

Sugarbread stole around the side of the house and headed toward the woods. I was close behind.

Doni was waiting on the porch with the infant in her arms when Sheriff Boggs pulled up with Granny Jack beside him.

"Mawnin' Doni. Need to see Champ."

"He done gone in de swamp, Mr. Sheriff."

"When do you 'spect him back, Doni?" Granny Jack asked.

"I don't rightly know. Sugarbread come running and say de law was after Champ. He ain't waste no time and took out fo' de swamp."

"Best send them boys in and git 'im," he said to Granny Jack, indicating Sugarbread and me. "It'll be a lot better'n if I hafta bring in the dawgs and flush 'im out."

"Otis, I want as much time as you can 'llow. I know you're shorthanded," Granny Jack requested.

"The army's done heah from the fort, Miz Jack, and they'll give me as many men as necessary ta git this taken care of."

Our mission into Willow Swamp to find Champ was eventually successful. We sent a periodic "whoooo!" ahead as we traced our path among the meandering branches and into the dense woods that canopied the main course of the swamp. A soft "whooo!" from behind startled us but brought our search to an end.

"I heard y'all coming through de woods and letcha pass on by to make sho' nobody's comin' long behind," Champ said.

"Daddy, de sheriff say he gonna bring in de dawgs if'n you don't come out de swamp. Say you done poisoned de men wid dat pie and you runnin' 'way done prove it."

"Ain't no poison in dat pie. Doni jes cook dat pie yestidday."

"They don't know it for sure," I interjected. "Doctor Connor told the sheriff that might be what killed the men."

"Colored folk ain't got no chance when dey git 'cused o' sump-in. Ain't nobody gonna lissen to no colored man. Done made up dey minds and ain't nuttin' gonna change 'em. Best thing a colored man kin do is jump de train and git as far 'way as he kin. Tell Miz

Jack I'se sorry but I can't let 'em put me in no jail. And tell 'er I ain't poisoned dat pie."

"But . . . Daddy!" Sugarbread protested.

"Now, you do like I say. You and Cephas gotta take care o' things. Jes' tell 'em you ain't seed me nowheah in de swamp."

The black Buick was gone when we emerged from the woods to tell Doni about not finding Champ.

"You look through de whole swamp?" she asked.

"We went all de way to Mr. Sligh's fence and ain't seed no sign of 'im."

"I hope he done run off wheah nobody gonna find 'im. Miz Jack gone wif de sheriff to Norway ta check on de men. 'Spec dey'll be back after 'while. Got some dinna for y'all waitin' back in de kitchin."

\* \* \*

We ate in a rush as usual, intent on getting a view of the buzzard chick with Champ gone.

Our suspicions had been confirmed after Champ told us he found the baby buzzard in the barn. He demanded that we leave the fledgling beast alone. To his eye, the buzzard was a partner on the farm, a reconnoiterer unequaled at finding animals that had strayed and fallen victim to wild dogs or hunters, a scavenger who slowly but completely cleared the landscape of all traces of decaying animal remains.

After Champ told us about the buzzard chick, we studied the buzzard hen's movement, noting the time from her departure until her return, when she squeezed through a hole at the end of the barn.

We watched her soar away across the cotton field and knew she would be gone sufficiently long for us to find the chick.

All was quiet inside as we creaked the barn door open, then closed it behind us to prevent Doni from knowing about our intrusion. Light filtered through the holes and missing boards. Nothing moved inside. Granny Jack's last buggy was thickly covered with dust and straw, the left wheel substantially bent with broken spokes and the axle shorn free of its attachment to the carriage—the relics of Granny Jack's last buggy ride. By the popular narrative, she had lost control of Roxie after forcing her through Moss Creek, then cussed her steadily until she separated from the buggy, which careened into a twenty-inch pine.

"Heah, buzzard," we called quietly in the stillness.

Our eyes scanned the rafters and the junk that had accumulated on the shelves over the years. Nothing moved.

"I see 'im," Sugarbread whispered, pointing to an indistinct black mass in the back corner.

"Be careful. Let's get 'im from both sides," I suggested.

We separated and eased along the sides of the buggy toward the back of the barn. I squeezed between the broken wheel and the buggy seat, keeping alert for any movement of the dark body. The buggy springs squeaked a bit under my weight.

"Shh!" whispered Sugarbread, just before a downy white buzzard chick fluttered from underneath the buggy seat, spewing carrion from his beak. It scored a direct hit; the vomitus covered Sugarbread's front before the putrid hose was turned on me as I struggled to untangle myself from the carriage wheel. Some of the slimy mess landed in the edge of my mouth as it gaped open in the initial fright.

The agitated, gawking chick turned, and in a couple violent heaves, shared a last spattering of his odorous weapon with Sugarbread. It then backed to the rear of the buggy, staring alternatively at Sugarbread and me with beak gaping, poised to repeat the full fury of its attack if necessary. It wasn't.

We both clambered for the barn door, spitting foul traces of carrion and wiping the mess from our clothes. We continued across the field, down the path to the creek and into the swimming hole, clothes and all.

We began working on a story as we scrubbed our bodies and hair and clothes: we went back into the swamp to find Champ and fell in as we were trying to swing across the water on a vine. It shouldn't be hard to believe. We had returned home in this shape many times before. Hopefully the residual odor that we brought in would be mistaken for swamp mud.

The experience gave me the idea for a prank to outshine all the prior harassment directed toward Miz Padgett by the white school-age kids of Neeses.

Her house was a veritable fortress, located half a block from the icehouse. A rhododendron hell entangled a hogwire fence along the street side, obscuring any view of her house and forming an impregnable wall. The only views of her house were over two boarded gates, one that gave entrance to a curved pebble walkway leading to the screened front porch, the other a double swinger that she used on the rare occasions she took her Chevrolet out from the shed beside her house. She walked to her teaching responsibilities at school—the distance of about a mile—and to church, which was much closer.

The rear approach to her fortress would have been equally formidable except that Carroll Westberry's garage backed up to her lot. We could drop into Miz Padgett's back yard from his roof. Escape would pose some problem if we were detected, but we could flee over the front gates if the plan broke down.

Two things were needed. A dead animal, preferably one dead for four or five days, ripe with the odors of rotting flesh. And the buzzard chick. Carroll Westberry and Jake Hutto would be good comrades in the undertaking. For several years they had understudied with the teenagers who were intent on assaulting Miz Padgett's place. Jake had further reason to help. He had repeatedly been subjected to Miz Padgett's "ruler" paddlings and had barely escaped repeating her third grade English class with a "low D-minus."

Procuring a dead animal for the buzzard chick would pose no great problem. I imagined that we could use innards from an animal butchered at Chaplin Brothers' store, but that would be too easily connected to us. It would be difficult to consider killing a dog, even someone else's dog. A cat was the most appropriate candidate. They were plentiful and dispensable—perhaps we would take one of our own.

Getting the buzzard chick's cooperation was another matter. Capturing him without a repeat of the first confrontation would be no easy undertaking. Sugarbread, I reasoned, would help me secure the services of the chick, though he knew he could not participate in the scheme at Miz Padgett's house. Colored boys didn't pull pranks on white people, not even Miz Padgett.

We would first poke at the buzzard chick through a hole in the barn, enticing it to spill its stomach's contents. Once emptied of the awful stuff, the chick would be vulnerable to attack with the help of a croker sack. After holding the bird without food all afternoon, we would deposit it at Miz Padgett's back door, its leg tied to the porch and with a ripe cat at its side for an odorous feast.

Imaging the scene as Miz Padgett opened her back door to encounter the buzzard chick dominated the recesses of my mind. I couldn't wait to recruit Carroll and Jake. Best of all would be the chance to view it all from the platform high atop the windmill in Carroll's back yard.

* * *

Every season found me in trees: tall straight poplars and hickories that challenged my arboreal abilities, stout-limbed gums loaded with bullaces, cantilevered cottonwoods draped with vines that carried me across the creek, and limber saplings whose tops could be bent to the ground. My favorite was a sprawling oak that stood alone in the pasture that stretched from the house eastward past a chicken house and a row of four peach trees to the woods that surrounded Grandpa Will's boiling springs. Before March, the sturdy lower limbs, naked except for balls of mistletoe at the tips, rambled almost perpendicularly from a massive rugated trunk. Once the skeleton was fleshed over with small leaves, it became a summer hideaway, a vantage from which I could survey all of our front acreage and not be seen; a listening post from which I could interlope in the affairs of the creatures below.

On the way home from the buzzard chick encounter, I needed to be cradled in the massive arms of my oak. I lay along the lowest limb with a view toward home punched through the green canopy. A gentle breeze rustled the leaves around me and carried away the odor that lingered in my clothes. I held to the limb as the security that had come to encompass me in recent months seemed to be slipping away.

Guineas plodded about beneath me, their long necks bent to the ground, keeping contact with their fellows with an occasional "p'track, p'track." Guineas enjoyed a privilege extended to none of the other farm animals. Granny Jack kept them and protected them merely because she enjoyed having them around. Their meat was dense and tough, and the eggs, which were usually deposited in inaccessible places, were so small they were worthless in bartering. Yet Granny Jack hatched a few eggs each year to replace guineas that drifted away or were caught by foxes.

In early spring we watched intently for their nesting places. Possession of a guinea egg assured success in the egg cracking contests of Easter. Whether cracking points or butts, chicken eggs posed no match for the tiny, thick-shelled opponents.

Most of the farm animals had given Sugarbread and me ample opportunity to witness the reproductive process from beginning to end. But guineas yielded not a single clue. They were as secretive as people. The whole process was secure with them. If all reproduction depended on learning how to do it from guineas, life on earth would have ceased with but a single generation.

I wished that all my searching for a llama had been successful. I'd inquired at every stock sale we attended in nearby Springfield, but none of the sellers knew the whereabouts of llamas. "Pain" Griffin, the stockyard's elderly but lightning-fast auctioneer, had seen just about everything on legs pass beneath his hammer in the bidding lot. In all his years, he had never seen a single llama. So, like the Indians who'd once resided in this very place, llamas remained creatures of my fantasy, possessed of virtues and endowments conjured on many a lonely day, the unknowing objects of my deepest affection.

I hoped Champ had made it aboard a train southbound or northbound that would carry him to safety in some promised land. He could become, I imagined, a colored Mr. Sif, a man with no family and no past. A new people would come to depend on his knowledge of how to handle mules, and tend to crops, and raise a family. He would be free of Pearl and Queenie.

I worried that Henny lay cold and dead and alone in some back room at Norway Camp. I might never again see him drop to one knee to show me a rock he had found, or feel his long fingers tousle my hair, or know the security of his hold on Pearl until I could pull myself onto her broad shoulders, or hear "Ja!" as he recoiled from my zinger.

# CHAPTER TWELVE

The *Times and Democrat.* "With The Allied Expeditionary Force (AEF)." June 29, 1944.

    With the AEF in Italy, June 4—(Delayed)—(AP, by Kenneth L. Dixon)—There is a little glade in the Alban Hills that must have been a pleasant place to know before the war rolled over it. An old-style Connecticut stone fence runs along its left bank and there is deep shade for a hundred yards from the short-lived vine that comes down from the slope and holds the scene together. . . .

    It is not so lovely now. The stone fence has been mutilated by mortar fire and the shade trees have been half shot down by the inexorable crush of artillery and the earth is torn and wounded so that it can never be quite the same again.

    It was here that one of the most melancholy and futile and yet perhaps valorous single actions of the entire Italian campaign was fought.

    It was fought by just two men and when I walked into the glade the men were still there—both dead. One was an American and the other a German and the evidence pointed surely to a mortal duel which destroyed both, yet exemplified the high type of devotion to duty that is something quite aside from the suicidal fanaticism practiced by the Japanese.

The German was lying with his feet to the little stream and with his head toward the center of the clearing. He lay on his left side with a machine pistol caught loosely in his arms and his right hand had relaxed only a little from the trigger guard so that you knew he died trying.

Head on toward him and less than 10 feet away lay the American. The German machine pistol had killed him as surely as a grenade from the dying American's hand had torn the life out of the German. . . .

I was there when the aid men came and took the American and German away. I saw the American's dog-tag and some of the things he carried in his pockets. I made a note of them. Some day when the war is over I want to write a letter to a young man who is now only three years old. I sort of think he'd like to know how his old man died.

\* \* \*

With the death of POW John Schyler, the Branch Camp at Norway joined the growing ranks of POW camps whose record had become marred by murder. War Department officials were becoming increasingly frustrated at the camps' inability to provide for the safety of the prisoners. They feared that each death provided the pretext for reprisals against Americans—now numbering over 80,000 held in German prisons.

The War Department was fully aware that hostilities might face the POWs in the United States, but it was ill prepared to accommodate the number of prisoners coming under its charge. Every available ship returning from the African and Mediterranean war zones was loaded with POWs. The numbers arriving on American soil had swollen from 5,000 in April 1943 to 170,000 by Christmas, and to 200,000 six months later. Among the numbers were more than 100,000 from Rommel's Afrika Korps, including entire companies that had been captured or had surrendered.

Every military base and Civilian Conservation Corps site had to be considered as a potential POW camp. Neither option was ideal. Base commanders argued against housing the prisoners, fearing that critical training and staging operations could be interrupted, and warned that juxtaposing POWs so close to US troops would jeopardize the safety of both. Residents in the vicinities of CCC campsites, concerned less about the safety of the POWs, were alarmed by the prospect of escapees disturbing their quiet, rural communities.

Providing security for the POWs loomed as a problem greatly exceeding the matter of providing shelter. The POW camps became dumping grounds for officers whose careers were going nowhere, soldiers who were mentally or physically unfit, retirees, social misfits, and those with combat injuries that precluded return to the front. The smattering of able soldiers among the guards were angered by the circumstance that had them babysitting POWs rather than tasting the blood and guts action for which they had enlisted. Few guards were sympathetic to the plight of the POWs: a life of adequate shelter, prepared meals, recreation, and entertainment was a life far better than that of either US or German troops at the front.

From the summer of 1943, when POW numbers began to swell, camp commanders from Carolina to California had been contending with a tide of POW beatings, killings, and "suicides." Hampered by the language barrier and inadequate personnel, they were woefully ineffective in the investigation of crimes of any sort.

At Aiken Side Camp, less than twenty miles from Norway, Horst Gunther was found hanging from a telephone pole. Gunther, an enlisted private from Ostfildern, had been captured near the end of the African campaign. He had been sent temporarily from Fort Gordon, Georgia, to Aiken for a labor detail. The guards considered him to be least likely to attempt an escape or

ROGER STEVENSON

to be involved in any type of altercation. He had taken a liking to American jazz and appeared comfortable with the guards and fellow POWs. Rumors circulated about camp that he had been condemned by a kangaroo court held by a clique of hardcore Nazis for becoming "Americanized" and for consorting with the enemy. Two sergeants, Erick Gauss and Rudolf Straub, were suspected of strangling Gunther and then hanging him from a telephone pole to suggest a suicide.

With the exception of an attempt to torch a locked barracks housing POWs in Illinois, the poisoning incident at Norway was distinctive in that it was directed at multiple prisoners. Certain camps had experienced the misfortune of several POW deaths, but they appeared to fit no pattern and were considered unrelated. Knifing, battering, and hanging each claimed its share of the victims. There followed each incident an almost universal failure to identify a perpetrator. Perhaps more consistent and curious was the strange sense of calm that settled over the camps' populations, guards and prisoners alike, in the aftermath of a killing.

Norway camp officials and MPs from Fort Jackson had become locked in conflict over the investigation of the sick men. Lab tests were still being conducted, but no one had any doubt that the men of Tent Eight had been poisoned. Captain Taylor casually questioned whether and to what extent the poisonings needed to be investigated.

"There's a war going on here. If a few of 'em die, that's less Krauts to feed and worry about," he suggested.

"That may be the case, but General Richart wants a full investigation," stated Sergeant Jansen, the head investigator from Fort Jackson. "He doesn't want the Germans to have any grounds for killing American men they are holding."

Sergeant Jansen wanted to be satisfied that the poisonings had not come from within. His office was still involved in investigating the death of Horst Gunther at Aiken and had been alerted to recent incidents at other camps where POWs had been beaten, stabbed, or hanged. Camp commanders were demanding that the cases be solved, but investigators had run into an impenetrable curtain of silence surrounding the prisoners. Nazis and antinazis alike said nothing in the wake of a death.

Sheriff Boggs found the arguments amusing. "Ya got this colored whose kid's been killed fighting the Nazis less than two weeks ago. He brings these men food, and they all die or git sick. Don't see any reason to suspect anybody else. Besides, he's took off on the run. Seems to me like an open-and-shut case."

"Well, that's part of the problem we got here, Sheriff," Aiken responded. "One of the Krauts didn't get sick."

"Bring Stauss back in and let's go over it again."

Henny entered the small room beside Captain Taylor's office, crisply groomed and wearing fresh PW garments. He was reminded of his interrogators' names and introduced to Sheriff Boggs.

"Stauss," Sergeant Jansen began, "we want to hear about last night again. We want to hear every detail you remember from the time you returned to camp. Let's start there: your arrival at camp from the Livingston farm."

"Ve all arrived from the farm, took ein beer at the canteen, and went to our tent to change for soccer."

"Who had the pie, and where was it during this time?"

"Champ, the helper on the farm, gave the pie to Wilhelm, and he took it to our tent before joining us at the canteen."

"What did you do after soccer?"

"I showered and went to supper."

"Were all the men of Tent Eight at supper?"

"Yes, ve all ate together."

"And then?"

"I went to the movie in the canteen. I think some went to read. I'm not sure where everyone went. But at the bugle ve all returned to the tent and ve all had a piece of the pie."

"Everyone ate the pie?"

"Everyone had a piece. Wilhelm cut the pie and everyone took a piece. It is all gone."

"What did you do after the pie?"

"I went to bed, but several of the men read or wrote letters. I was sleepy after the movie."

"What happened next?"

"I think John was first to become sick. He slept in the bunk above me. John Schyler—there are two Johns in our tent. At first, I didn't think much about it because he becomes sick so easily. Sometimes he vomits on the truck to the farm. On the ship from Africa and on the train from Norfolk he was sick all the way. Even after he began to bleed, I thought it was from vomiting so much. Then Wolf became sick, and then Enno, I believe, and then Wilhelm. Frederick vomited blood the first time.

"When everyone became sick, I went for the guard," Henny continued. "He seemed scared and turned his rifle on me and told me to halt. I told him the men were bleeding and he told me to stand there until another guard arrived."

"And a second guard came?"

"Yes, I think from the back tower, but it was a long time. I could hear the men behind me retching. When the doctor came, John—John Schyler—was already dead."

"And through all of this you never felt sick?"

"Nein. I kept expecting it, but I never felt sick."

"And you ate the pie?"

"Ja, just like everyone else."

"And never got sick?"

"Nein, not at all."

"Perhaps, Stauss, you never became sick, because you poisoned the other men."

"Nein, they are my friends."

"Are you a Nazi?"

"I was a Nazi, from my youth."

"Did you serve in the Hitler Youth?"

"Ja, from age fourteen years."

"And did you swear allegiance to Hitler and to Germany?"

"Ja, I did."

"And did you poison these men for the Fuehrer?"

"Nein, I did not poison."

"What others in Tent Eight are Nazis?"

"Wilhelm—Wilhelm is the only one, I think."

"And Wilhelm is sick?"

"Ja, he became sick soon after John and Wolf."

"And you never felt sick?"

"I didn't feel good with everyone around me vomiting. But I did not vomit, and I did not bleed."

"Do you know, Stauss, that Enno has applied to stay in America when the war is over?"

"I knew that he wanted to."

"And that bothered you, didn't it, Stauss?"

"Nein, I did not care if that was his decision."

"Stauss, you write letters to Berlin every week, do you not?"

"Ja, I write to my family."

"And you have told your 'family' about Enno wanting to stay in America?"

"I have probably mentioned it."

"We think you have indeed mentioned it. In fact, you noted it in great detail in two letters dated May 22 and June 6. We find it strange that you do not receive letters back from Berlin, Stauss. Only the occasional letter from Darmstadt."

"My family, I mean my wife, is in Berlin."

"In your Soldbuch ID, you give Darmstadt as home. Which is it Stauss, Berlin or Darmstadt?"

"My family, my parents, are in Darmstadt, but my wife is in Berlin."

"And not a single letter from your wife even though you've been writing her every week?"

"I cannot explain. I fear something has happened to her. We lost our son, and she was very despondent when we talked last in November."

"Let me tell you, Stauss, how I got it figured. You write letters every week to Berlin, but they go to German authorities and not to your wife. You transmit information on the other prisoners. Anyone who reads American magazines. Anyone who talks to the guards. Anyone who gets lax in your ramrod salute. Anyone who says anything about Hitler. . . ."

\* \* \*

Sheriff Boggs passed through the farm several times during the following week, once in the Buick and on other occasions beside a deputy in a marked Ford, stopping to talk with Granny Jack or Doni if they happened to be in sight, and otherwise scanning the fields and feed lots before departing. Granny Jack suspected that he was looking for evidence that Champ was hidden somewhere on the farm.

Flames lapped against the black kettle that formed the centerpiece of the clothes washing operation set up next to the well, adding to the heat of the midmorning sun. Granny Jack took each piece of clothing through a sequence of soaking, rubbing along the ribs of a scrub board, plunging in the boiling water with a broom handle, and dunking in two tubs of rinse water, before hanging them on a rope stretched between the well post and a hickory tree beside the hog lot. She straightened up from the scrub tub as the marked Ford eased off the road and Sheriff Boggs walked toward her.

"Mawnin, Miz Jack."

"Mawnin, Sheriff. You got some news for us?"

"Yep. That Stauss that worked for you really took a grilling and the young sergeant from Fort Jackson figured they had their man, though he never admitted anything. Locked him up 'til the lab tests came back.

"Turned out to be Wilhelm, that shortest one. 'Pears he's a Nazi that's been spying on the other men all along. Best we can tell, he became depressed about all the news reports of Allied successes against Hitler and was angered by the other fellows becoming comfortable and converted by American propaganda."

"But I thought he was sick with the rest of 'em."

"He put on a good show, but the lab couldn't find a trace of arsenic in his blood."

"What about Henny?"

"They released him this morning. Looked like he might have been involved at first. He was telling the truth 'bout not getting sick. He removed the meringue from the top before eating the pie. That's 'parently where Wilhelm sprinkled the arsenic. The cook verified that Henny doesn't eat eggs. Always scrapes them off his plate. They's no reason Henny can't come back to work if you need him."

"I do need him, but I need Champ more."

"I almost forgot to tell you. The MPs in Columbia pulled Champ off a northbound freight car. He's been sitting in jail in Columbia all this time. Wouldn't tell 'em his name or anything. Matched the description we'd sent out. My men'll pick him up first chance we git."

# CHAPTER THIRTEEN

The *Times and Democrat*. "Hot Contest Between Wallace and Truman for Second Place Develops—Vote on Vice Presidency Put Over Until Friday By Party Leaders." July 21, 1944.

Chicago Stadium, July 20—(AP)—From a Pacific Coast Naval Base, President Roosevelt accepted a fourth term nomination tonight and told a wartime Democratic national convention—and Americans—to take a look at the record and then determine whether to entrust a worldwide job "to inexperienced and immature hands. . . ."

"Complete victory within the next four years seems wholly likely," the President said. Then in what appeared to be an assurance that he would not seek a fifth term but would "retire to the quiet of a private life," he added:

"In any event, new hands will then have full opportunity to realize the ideals which we seek."

Apparently epitomizing his own personal platform for the battle to keep Governor Thomas E. Dewey of New York out of the White House, Mr. Roosevelt outlined a three-point world-wide job for 1944:

"First, to win the war—to win it fast, to win it overpoweringly.

"Second, to form worldwide international organizations, and to arrange to use the armed forces of the sovereign nations of the world to make another war impossible within the foreseeable future.

"Third, to build an economy for our returning veterans and for all Americans—which will provide employment and decent standards of living. . . ."

"The war waits for no elections," Mr. Roosevelt said. "Decisions must be made—plans must be laid—strategy must be carried out. They do not concern merely a party or a group."

\* \* \*

Dog days dragged by with few obligations. The last arsenic and molasses applications had been made and the cotton bolls were expanding to Granny Jack's satisfaction. Corn tasseled out, the ears grew to a good size, and the stalks browned in the dry heat.

Hummingbirds returned as they did each summer, daily paying a call to the flowering thistle beside the back porch, reestablishing their territory and driving away intruders to this favorite spot of nectar. On the first morning visits, their ruby throats blazed against a background sparkling with dew. Their aerial acrobatics rivaled those of the bats that thatched the air as evening approached. Neither could be hit by a thrown rock, but neither could evade a precisely aimed sling shot. Granny Jack disapproved of both types of attack.

Bullaces were beginning to ripen and enticed Sugarbread and me more frequently into vines high in the gum and oak trees in search of the black delicacies. Plums and peaches and blackberries were plentiful. Granny Jack and Doni put up dozens of jars of jelly. Cantaloupes and citron and watermelons were picked as needed.

Granny Jack decided early in the spring to have one POW help Champ every day and to use the other men only when the work demanded additional hands. The three-member crew would be needed for weeks at a time, she thought, to both pull corn and chop, poison, and pick cotton. Henny came alone in the weeks that intervened. Except for the few days that Granny Jack wanted his help around her home, he stayed in Champ's company doing whatever Champ directed. In addition, he took over the routine of handling the mules.

Late one day that Henny came alone, he rode Pearl around the perimeter of the cleared land before turning her into the lot for feeding.

"I ain't never seen nothing like it," Champ remarked when Henny took his first ride. "I'll work 'em sunup t' sundown, but you ain't getting me on top of nery one of 'em."

Champ had grumbled about the grey mules since the day they arrived. When breaking ground, they pulled beyond the corner or short of it, necessitating that Champ wrestle the heavy plow into realignment at every turn. They trampled the cotton at the end of the rows and required constant geeing and hawing to keep them off the plants even on a straight row. They balked at every stream, no matter how small—even at a dry creek bed. They resisted working alone. When separated to pull a single plow each, they neighed constantly. But worst of all was the fact that Champ was unable to say he could ride them.

Champ had been on top of Queenie once before . . . briefly. He had agreed to try to ride her at Melvin's urging. After mounting her from the barn door, she bolted free of Melvin's hold on the bridle and, in a single convulsion, threw Champ through the barbed wire enclosure.

Champ longed to have again the team of black mules that Granny Jack had traded away. He particularly missed Roxie. She'd had only a fraction of Pearl's strength and plodded at her own slow pace, but she understood what she was doing. She'd kept in the furrow and could pull the length of a field with no corrections. Granny Jack had exercised some revenge in selling Roxie, as she was also the mule who had run away with her at the reigns, totaling her buggy.

Henny and Champ found adequate work to occupy their time together. After the last poisoning of the cotton, they hauled a load of logs to the sawmill and sawed enough boards to repair the barn and Champ's house. They cut wagonloads of red oak to split and stack for winter's firewood.

When Champ put work aside and went fishing, Henny was allowed to do the same.

Sugarbread and I labored off and on at restoring the dam of gum logs and earth that forced water beyond our swimming hole and into the banks on each side. Lily pads and ferns thrived in the shallows. Along the face of the dam, the sandy bottom was deep enough to accommodate our belly-flop style of diving.

Throughout the summer we added load after load of dirt to the center of the dam to protect against a thunderstorm heavy enough to force the creek through our handiwork. Champ spent one day showing us how to construct a spillway across one end of the dam.

We would shed our clothes on the dam with little concern that anyone would disturb our privacy. Occasionally Granny Jack or Doni would cross our dam on a shortcut between the farmhouses. We feigned protest as they passed but kept our nude bodies submerged.

Sugarbread and I were both boney, ribs and pelvis protruding and little padding anywhere. Our scrawniness was not for lack of plenty to eat at both houses. Doni said she reckoned we just ran it all off.

"You gittin' black as Sugarbread!" Doni yelled at me one day. "And you jest as scrawny."

Granny Jack and Doni were the only ones concerned about our safety in the swimming hole. They held that we should not go near the water until we knew how to swim.

The long foreskin that dangled from the end of Sugarbread's penis, and the absence of a covering over mine, was the subject of repeated discussions.

"What happened to the end o' yo' dong?" Sugarbread had inquired when we first started swimming together in the nude.

"Doc Connor got it, I think," I answered.

Doctor Connor had brought circumcision to Neeses.

Just about everyone knew about circumcision from the Bible

and little objection was raised to its widespread adoption. A full generation, including all of Granny Jack's sons, had been subjected to the ritual. If Doctor Connor happened to make it to the birth of a male baby, or if he were called in for any reason during the first week of life, loss of the prepuce to his pearl-handled pocket-knife was assured.

"Yo' dong ain't got no pertekshun," Sugarbread observed. "Don't it get sore rubbin' on yo' britches?"

"Sometimes, but most times it just feels good."

\* \* \*

Never was the farm lacking in an abundant supply and variety of bait for fishing. Champ was basically a blue worm fisherman. He gave insects, animal entrails, fatback, and crickets their due, but blue worms were always easy to find in the mud bogs along the creek bottom, and they yielded consistent success in his hands. Mr. Sif swore similarly by the drone larvae he stole from his beehive.

An audubon of juicy delicacies were at our disposal. Plump white giant worms could be found in the creases of rotting wood. Grasshoppers, particularly those with yellow underwings, populated the grasses and the corn fields. Crickets were plentiful under every brush pile and along the brick base of the well. Tomato worms had their season while the leaves were young and tender.

For several summers, Sugarbread and I had been hooked on catawba worms. Uncle Jme had told us about using catawbas to pull two-pound redbreasts out of Willow Swamp, and even larger ones from the South Edisto.

"Those redbreasts, now, they're the slickest of all the fish and the best in the pan," he had told us. "They'll back up under a log and sit there and watch worms and crickets drift by all day long. But the juicy catawba—well, the redbreast just can't refuse 'em."

Uncle Jme had given me my first lesson in handling catawbas. He tapped a cane along a limb of the catalpa that grew near the side door of his mercantile, while I quickly gathered the few worms that fell to the ground.

"The secret's in the turning. If the catawba ain't turned, it ain't no better'n having any ole worm."

With a knife, he slit the head and then telescoped the worm end to end with a matchstick.

I'd sat on the sidestep for a while, cutting heads and pushing. In the end, my hands were black with their juices, my shirt and face splattered.

Catawbas first made their appearance each year in the patches of silk veil scattered about the foliage of the catalpa tree. They emerged as tiny pale green worms and rapidly dispersed to every leaf on the tree. Catalpas grew along our roadside and behind the barn at Champ's place. Even though the womenfolk complained about the odor of the leaves, no one ever seriously threatened the catalpas. They were nurtured with the same care as the fig trees that found residence on the southern face of every farmhouse in the area.

In the summer, the catalpas' heart-shaped leaves were systematically stripped by—and in the process turned into—an army of engorged, blackish-green worms.

Sugarbread and I monitored our trees daily from the first of August. It took only a few days after the worms' appearance until they ripened into the ultimate redbreast lures. Fortunately, they came during dog days, when the motivation for work had ebbed and the crop situation was not compelling. Even the work that should be done in summer could be set aside for a while. Corn could be pulled at leisure and cotton had not yet begun to open.

Our first harvest of catawbas was carefully bagged and hung on the side of the barn in readiness for contest with the redbreasts in Willow Swamp.

"Bring back a good mess of 'em," Granny Jack said as I headed out to meet Champ and Henny and Sugarbread. "Let Champ keep any horny heads and catfish. I don't want to mess with them."

As excited as I was about being with Champ with his decades of experience fishing in Willow Swamp, I wished even more that Henny would be the adult beside me, alone or with Sugarbread.

Champ selected the first black hole we came to on the main

branch in Willow Swamp. He snapped the head from a catawba, and with a single swift movement pushed the worm's tail through the opening with a stick, slid a hook through the black mass, spit on it, and eased it into the entrance to the pothole. He wiped the slime on his britches leg and settled quietly onto the bank.

Trying not to acknowledge the abandon with which Champ had turned the catawba, I headed downstream.

"Y'all need any help with the worms?" Champ asked.

"No, I know how to turn 'em," I responded.

"Okay. Jes' watch out for cottonmouths. I'll come on afta' I fish out dis hole."

We followed the main tributary as it snaked itself into the underbush ahead and were quickly out of Champ's sight. We passed several tolerable locations before coming to a brush pile with foam eddying against it.

"Why don't you take this hole, Henny?" I suggested. "Slide yo' line in and let it drift up under those bushes. And keep teasin' 'em," I added. "Don't let yo' catawba stay in the water too long. If they don't hit it, pull it out and let it drift to the hole again. When they hit it, you got to yank it quick or they'll tie you 'round a root."

"Turning catawbas is a snap," I assured Henny, pulling out my small Barlow, a present Miz Hattie Padgett gave each of the boys who completed her third-grade class. "You just make a slit across the tail like this and push him through," I explained as I attempted to use a twig to telescope the worm's head. The juices squirted and ripped as I pushed, and the progress of turning the insides out halted about midway along the worm.

"This sometimes happens," I explained to Henny, not yet totally discouraged. After first breaking my plunger stick, I then tried to force the head on through, stabbing my finger in the process. After a failed attempt to hook the turned portion and pull it over the unturned end, I felt as much a novice as I had sitting on Uncle Jme's side stairs, covered in black goo. The only recourse was to either grasp the oozing, partially turned worm and try to complete the turning, or to hook the half-turned worm and just start fishing.

"Perhaps ve should push them the other way," Henny suggested, noting my failure.

"You can do 'em any way you want," I replied, handing Henny my Barlow and taking my partially turned catawba to the next turn in the swift water.

Willow Swamp seemed entirely untouched by humans. Lush vegetation sprang from all sides, the tangles making some areas impenetrable. The swamp's floor was strewn with flowers and shrubs I never saw on the higher farmlands. All was still except for the ripple of flowing water and an occasional flicker of a woodpecker through the trees.

The redbreasts didn't disappoint us, taking the catawbas with determination. When pulled out of their lairs, they rippled across the water's surface, racing to the line's limit in one direction and then the other. They gave only a moment before dragging the line around brush or roots and freeing themselves.

Sugarbread and Henny and I fished along together, moving farther and farther from the place we'd left Champ. Henny was quick to set the hook after a strong bite and lost fewer redbreast than Sugarbread and me. In the process of trying to find redbreast holes, we caught several catfish and brim, and Sugarbread caught a small eel, which we thought at first was a snake.

Henny and I sat for a while together on the bank after we'd used up all the catawbas. I lay back against a cypress tree in the warmth that filtered through the swamp's tall canopy.

"Did you ever see Hitler?" I asked.

"Sure, since my childhood. Everyvone in Germany saw him. He vas everyvere. Ve vere proud to call ourselves Germans. He made us that vay. Ve vanted to vork for the country and for Hitler."

"Did you go fishing back home?"

"Ja, our farm was in the Rhine Valley, and ve enjoyed fishing in the river and tributaries."

"Did you have catawbas?"

"Nein, I haf not seen them before. Ve used minnows in the river, not flies. My father kept a boat, which he took us on during the veekends."

"Do you have a girlfriend?"

"Nein, I have a vife, Kari."

"And kids—" I began to ask. But the flitting about of small birds in the underbrush and the rushing of water had obscured movement in the woods behind us, and we were startled by a high-pitched voice.

"Well, well. Lookie what we got heah!"

Henny and I turned at once, our eyes stopping initially at the barrels of a shotgun dangling down along mud-spattered britches, then up to the smiling face of Skeeter Williams. "Gotta be my lucky day, runnin' into a Natzi out heah in the middle of this 'Merican swamp," Skeeter continued.

"Mr. Skeeta, this is my Uncle Jme's land," I responded nervously, keeping my eye on the shotgun, still pointed at the ground.

"Now, boy, I'll tell you what you better do. You better git on back on the hill to yo' ole squaw."

"What you gonna do to Henny?" I asked.

"Just you never mind, and get on outta here. We just gonna take a little walk on down de swamp, together."

"I ain't goin' nowhere without Henny," I protested. I pulled up from the bank, catching my toe on a vine, and stumbled forward toward Skeeter.

He backed a few steps and raised the barrels toward my midsection.

"Drop it back down," came a familiar voice. Champ stood some few feet behind Skeeter, the butt of his cane pole pushed into his back. "I done seed you comin' through de swamp and know'd you be up to no good."

Skeeter lowered the barrel again, then dropped the gun onto the bank on Champ's further orders.

"Hand me dat gun, boy," Champ directed me. With the gun securely in hand, Champ instructed Skeeter, still held at bay with his fishing cane: "Mr. Skeeta, you better take off through dis swamp, and if you much as look back I'm gonna spray yo' hide with dis buckshot. Now, git 'way from heah."

Skeeter tore out, falling once in the underbrush but scrambling up and disappearing on the run.

"Yhoo, you got him good!" I congratulated Champ, hugging him around his broad middle.

"We may not be rid o' him," he responded. "We best git our things together and git back outta heah. He's likely got a still back in dese woods somewheah."

"But these woods belong to Uncle Jme," I said, denying the connection that Granny Jack had long suspected.

"Don't you nevermind 'bout dat. Y'all got any redbreast?"

"Ve got some good vones," Henny answered, pulling the string with our catch from the water.

"Let's get on out to de hill 'fo Skeeta come back in heah."

The walk home took over an hour, usually a tiring trip, but invigorated today by recalling our encounter with Skeeter. Sugarbread and I argued about who caught the biggest fish and looked for liverwort leaves to sell to Uncle Jme to mix with his pipe tobacco. Most of the way home, we could see a solitary buzzard circling in the distance, catching updrafts and taking long soaring paths across the horizon, eventually disappearing over the Elberta orchard as we neared Champ's house. I suspected we had not seen the last of Skeeter Williams.

# CHAPTER FOURTEEN

The *Times and Democrat.* "Hitler Tells About Attempt Made on Life. Himmler Given Orders to Exterminate All Opposition." July 21, 1944.

London, Friday, July 21—(AP)—Adolf Hitler, burned and bruised by a bomb explosion, told the world today that a group of German army officers attempted to assassinate him Thursday to prepare for surrender "as in 1918," but asserted the conspiracy had been nipped by speedy, ruthless action.

Shortly afterward it was announced officially that "the ringleaders either have been shot or committed suicide." Among those executed it said, was the man accused by Hitler of planting the bomb—Col. Count Von Stauffenberg.

Hitler called it the work of "a small clique of stupid officers," but implied strongly that it was actually a wide-open split in the German army and he outlined a broad and ruthless program to put down the incipient revolt.

He appointed Heinrich Himmler, chief of the dreaded Gestapo, to be Commander-in-Chief of the home front to exterminate all opposition "ruthlessly," and declared:

"I order that no military authority, no leader of any

unit, no soldier in the field, is to obey any order emanating from these usurpers.

"I also order that it is everyone's duty to arrest—or, if they resist, to kill on sight—anyone issuing or handing on such orders."

Speaking for six minutes in coldly furious tones, Hitler said he was "unharmed and well," even though a bomb had exploded within six feet of him and had injured 13 members of his personal military staff, one fatally. . . .

Reichmarshal Hermann Goering, beefy No.2 Nazi, went on the air immediately after his Fuehrer, declaring:

"A plot was made against our Fuehrer by a Col. Count Von Stauffenberg, at the order of a member of a clique of former generals, who were dismissed because of their cowardly and bad leadership.

"The Fuehrer was saved by providence."

* * *

Light flashed momentarily across the front window, then returned from the opposite direction to cast a steady beam across the foot of my bed. Soon there were three pairs of headlights directed at the house and several others scattering light into the woods. A rumble of men's voices slowly became audible as the engines idled.

My mind was racing at the sudden commotion outside. Prince added to the confusion, barking in a steady volley. Granny Jack had rolled out of her bed when Prince started barking and was searching about in the closet underneath the hall stairs.

For a bit, the voices remained at some distance, seemingly along the road about two hundred feet from the front of the house. From the position of the lights, I imagined the cars had been driven into the bed of marigolds Granny Jack had planted along the shoulder of the road. The figures cast shadows toward the house as they milled about, but I couldn't make out a single one.

Voices from their midst became more excited and the night exploded with light as flames engulfed a cross, which towered to a height of twelve or fifteen feet. Two figures in white robes and hoods stood out against the night, dramatically announcing their ignoble intent. I had never seen a Klansman before, but they fit my imagination sufficiently that I was left with no doubt. White robes made a line of ten or so figures visible in front of the flaming cross.

"Hey Mister Natzi, come on out heah," one voice beckoned.

"Yeah, Natzi, we got sum'n for you!" a second voice called. Prince fought the end of his chain and put up a noisy distraction from the end of the house.

"Hush that dog up," snarled a voice from the line of men.

"Hold on now—" said another. "You can't shoot the kid's dog."

But Prince lunged again and again until the chain gave way. He bolted directly toward the men, still barking furiously with teeth flashing.

"I'll git 'im!" yelled one of the men. A single shot pierced the night and Prince's bark was silenced as he tumbled across the front yard.

I ran for the door, but Granny Jack was already there, braced against it.

"But they shot Prince!" I yelled when she blocked me.

"You ain't going out there and git shot too," she stated. "Hold on before one of those jackasses loses his head." Granny Jack cautiously opened the door and took a single step onto the porch, holding her arm up in front of her eyes against the blinding lights.

"Listen here, you heath'ns, you git yo'self back off my property. I know every one of you."

"Now, Miz Jack, we ain't meaning no harm to you and the boy. We just want the Natzi."

"Yeah, git him on out heah," another demanded.

"You ain't gonna bother nobody. You get off my property," Granny warned again. "Skeeta, Skeeta Williams, you no-count, I know you're out there. You oughta be ashamed of yourself—every one of you."

"Listen, old woman. You just gonna get yourself hurt, and the boy too, if'n you don't do what we say."

"Just send that Natzi out heah. He's all we want."

My chest was heaving as I eased outside the door beside Granny Jack, who tried, too late, to push me back behind her. I broke free from her and ran into the yard to Prince.

I pulled him into my arms and sat in the sand, crying and trembling uncontrollably. Granny Jack repeatedly beckoned me to safety, but I was paralyzed with grief and anger.

Nothing made any sense to me—who the men were, why they thought anyone was with us, and what they were intent on doing. I only knew Prince lay in the yard before me and Granny Jack was angrier than I had ever imagined she could be.

Several of the men moved from the cross toward me. Before I could get to my feet, I was overwhelmed by a loud blast and felt a sting to my left ear that rippled across my face. A warm thickness oozed down the left side of my neck.

"Oh, shit!" were the only words I heard, before the men quieted and backed slowly toward the cross. One of the headlights directed at the house was now darkened. Then, with a sudden scramble, the night was filled with loud exclamations and slamming car doors. Engines revved and tires spun up a cloud of dust that swirled and settled around the cross. When I looked up, I saw Granny Jack on the porch with Grandpa Will's 12-gauge shotgun still braced against her shoulder—with one unspent chamber.

When the roar of engines was in the distance, I stood and cradled Prince's limp body in my arms. A warm mat of blood covered his right shoulder.

"Lay him up heah on the porch," Granny Jack instructed. She sounded exhausted.

"You never told me you could shoot that ole gun," I said.

"Your grandpa showed me how to shoot it, but in all these years, I never even thought about it. I hope I neva have to shoot it again. It still kicks like a mule. I guess I was too scared to remember that."

"I thought I'd got shot when I heard it go off," I added, as I held pressure to a nick on my ear from a link of Prince's chain.

My heart was still racing as I sat on the porch steps, rubbing Prince's fur. Granny Jack stood above me, shotgun under arm, her face lit by the still active flames before us. She looked ten feet tall.

"We'll bury him in the morning," Granny Jack said, putting a comforting hand on my shoulder.

"Were they afta Henny?" I asked.

"I 'spec so," Granny Jack responded. "They's all kinda rumors going 'round 'bout them prisoners, 'specially Henny staying heah. Miz Hattie told me she'd heard that one of 'em had taken up with Mamie."

"I ain't never been so scared. I still can't stop shaking."

"People git crazy sometimes," Granny Jack continued. "They git all worked up inside, and it don't take much for 'em to do something terrible."

"How'd you know Skeeta was out there?"

"I didn't know and I still don't know. But he was the most worthless person who came to mind. I thought calling out a name might make some difference."

"I bet he was out there, after what happened in the swa—" My thought was abruptly cut short by the whistling of britches legs and pounding of feet approaching the side of the house. Granny Jack swung the 12-gauge in that direction as Champ appeared at the corner of the porch.

"Nawsum, Miz Jack, don't shoot me!" called Champ.

Granny Jack dropped the muzzle to the porch floor, her usual tremor accentuated by the renewed excitement.

"I heard the shot and came a running fast as dese legs would move—" he started, then paused as a bristling of sparks and flames shooting from the cross drew his attention. "Lawd, look at dat cross! I ain't did nothing wrong, is I? Oh Lordy, Miz Jack, what's them folks doing 'round heah?"

"They are just up to the same old no-count tricks, Champ. They ain't got much to do, coming heah."

"They came after Henny, Champ," I added, "and Granny's done run 'em off with the shotgun." Now exhilarated in the old woman's accomplishment, I couldn't help boasting.

Champ's britches were wet up past the knees from running through the creek bed. The upper part of his clothes was equally wet from perspiration.

"Sit heah on the porch and rest, Champ," Granny Jack insisted.

"Nawsum. I spec' I better get back 'cross the creek if'n you be okay. Doni be worried to death some'n dun happened to you. If'n dey come back, you just fire that shotgun again and I'll come runnin'," he reassured.

"I don't think they will be back tonight. You get on back and tell Doni we're all right. You need to be heah before daybreak. Mr. Sif will be heah early and he's gonna want to shoot those stumps, too," Granny Jack reminded.

"Tell Sugarbread I'll see him in the morning," I called to Champ as he disappeared into the darkness beyond the porch.

Granny Jack and I sat on the steps, staring at the cross and recounting our fear.

The cross burned brightly for a while, then crashed forward, throwing sparks toward us and setting the grass in its path ablaze. The embers had almost all blackened before we returned to our beds and a restless night.

# CHAPTER FIFTEEN

The *Times and Democrat.* "Peas Found In Tut Tomb Flourish Upon Planting After Some 3,300 Years." August 11, 1944.

Orlando, Fla. August 6— (AP)—The second and third generations of three small dry peas, nearly 3,300 years old, are creating quite a stir in the Florida horticultural world. The peas were discovered in the tomb of King Tutankhamen among the precious works of art, jewels and rich furnishings befitting an Egyptian ruler of 1350 B.C.

In 1936, an English archaeologist who had worked on the Tutankhamen excavation sent three of these 33-century-old peas to his American friend, Maj. Walter G. Dyer, who in due season planted them in his garden at Portsmouth, R. I.

They flourished as any ordinary pea from a seed store and the resultant seeds planted the following year brought a harvest of about a pound and a half of fresh peas.

The major brought some of these seeds with him to the AAF tactical center here and the school commandant, Col. Harlan W. Holden, planted some 60 in the sand-based soil outside his office.

Florida gardeners raised their eyebrows at the colonel's planting peas in April since the pea bearing season is during December and early January. However, by early

June the plants were full grown at seven feet.

These green peas, which grow about four to six in a pod, are slightly longer, flatter and darker than the average garden variety. The pea vine bears a white wing-like flower which is a little smaller than the average. . . .

Maj. Dyer ate a part of the second crop, after boiling them in the usual manner. He says they were very tasty and had a distinctive walnut flavor. There is a possibility that these peas, more heat resistant and apparently more "bug-resistant" than the common pea, may prove the nucleus of a new southern crop.

\* \* \*

An unwritten rule on our farm was that each day could accommodate only a single endeavor. If Friday was the day to put up fences, nothing else would be accomplished that day. All hands set posts, pulled wire, and stapled. Any job worth doing was worth devoting to it a full day's work.

Mr. Sif quarreled with this philosophy whenever he came to help. He considered it essential to start a second job before knocking-off time.

As much as I saw of Mr. Sif, he remained a mystery. It was strange for a person to live in Neeses and not claim as kin someone else from the area. Yet Mr. Sif and his wife, Lillian, had arrived, raised a family, and so far as anyone knew, never received a visit from a relative. Nor did they ever take leave of Neeses to visit elsewhere. It was rumored that Mr. Sif was a man on the run for some unknown but vile deed committed in his youth, though no evidence ever surfaced to substantiate that or any of the other rumors that periodically circulated regarding his past. Mr. Sif never spoke of his background; nor had friends or whiskey ever coaxed a revelation from him.

If the townsfolk felt any uneasiness about his past, it was inconsequential. The town had come to depend on Mr. Sif, perhaps more so than on any of its native sons. He knew where every property line was supposed to be, when and by whom it was laid out, and where the markers could be found. He could step off an acre so close that no one argued once he set a stake. Never would a wellhole have to be dug twice if Mr. Sif rodded the site; nor would cotton and corn rows have to be reseeded if his suggested planting time was observed. His joints warned him of impending weather changes, a forecast he confirmed in the disposition and movement of the animals. His services were shared by the widow Jack, the colored sharecropper, and the prosperous cotton farmers alike.

Although Granny Jack had a considerable reservoir of farming savvy herself, she seemed to take comfort in knowing that Mr. Sif watched the progress on our place. He gave a hand at an endless number of tasks, from butchering meat to terracing the fields. If money ever passed to his hand for any of the work he performed, I never knew of it.

* * *

The sun rose as if the terrors of the previous night had never happened. From the kitchen table, I could see the heads of grey mules bobbing against the horizon beyond the back road to our house. Sugarbread sat alongside Champ on the wagon bench. Champ pulled the wagon around the house and tied the mules to a limb of the live oak next to the hog lot. Champ and Sugarbread unloaded tools and placed them beside one of the roots that radiated from the tree's massive trunk.

"Pull dose boards off de wagon and stack 'em next de fence dere, boy," Champ instructed Sugarbread. Then Champ took the axe and disappeared from sight around the front of the house.

I could hear repeated peals of the axe as Champ broke up the charred remains of the cross and dragged the pieces into the edge of the woods.

Mr. Sif and the PW truck arrived soon after from opposite directions. Henny jumped from the covered back, and after a brief exchange between Mr. Sif and the driver, the PW truck pulled away toward Neeses to deliver a few more workers.

"Mawnin' Champ."

"Mawnin' Mr. Sif."

"Mawnin' Henny, you gittin' 'customed to the farm work?"

"Ja, I like it okay. Champ shows me the work."

"Where is Cephas, Champ?" Mr. Sif asked as he began sharpening his pocketknife on a stone.

"Cephas fitted during the night and he be still in de bed. I brought Sugarbread along to help out some."

"If I 'da known that, Alec could have come along to help. I think we can manage though if Henny can give us a hand. He looks pretty stout."

"How many you think we got, Champ?"

"Miz Jack reckon'd she got eighteen. That ole biggest sow had nine males in her litter. Miz Jack wants to keep one for breeding. She got the best one penned up."

Late the previous spring, four litters had been born to our striped Hampshire sows. Two from one litter had died. One appeared to have been crushed by the sow; the second, a runt from birth, had been found dead in the food trough.

We were fixing the pigs unforgivably late this year. The young boars were now up to sixty or seventy pounds and consumed a significant portion of time attempting to mount the sows— and one another, after we'd segregated them.

Granny Jack had bred the sows as usual during the second week in the new year. By her account the litters would arrive in three months, three weeks, and three days from the date of breeding. This placed the births in early May, late enough that there was little likelihood of losing any of the litter to cold weather. She allowed the piglets to suckle for two months before weaning them to meal and corn. She liked to have the boars fixed soon after weaning but events of the summer had thrown much of her schedule askew.

Although I was not yet sure why we castrated the young male pigs, I witnessed the ritual annually. The first few times, it had bothered me to hear the pigs protesting, but with each passing year it became less and less offensive. The first cutting of the skin always seemed to bring the loudest squealing and struggling to get free. Thereafter, the pigs seemed resigned to some terrible ordeal and just snorted or flinched as Mr. Siff cut the other tissues and shelled out the testes.

"You gonna ketch'um or hold 'em?" Mr. Sif asked.

"Them boys'll ketch'em, and Mr. Henny'll help me throw 'em over de fence," said Champ. "We oughta be able to hold 'em down for ya.'"

Sugarbread and I scrambled about in the well-manured pen until we cornered one of the young boars, grabbed the hind legs, and struggled to drag him across the pen. It took us several minutes, slipping in the mud, bumping into each other, laughing, and losing our grip on the legs before we got him within Champ's reach. Once Champ grabbed ahold, though, he easily swung the struggling pig over the fence, put him down on the side, and rested a knee on its flanks with the testes exposed between the rear legs.

Henny flinched a bit as he helped Champ position the first pig for Mr. Sif. As the first cut was made, he paled, then released his grip on the head and front legs and ran to the fence.

"I still got 'im," Champ assured Mr. Sif, who continued the operation, barely looking up as Henny lost his breakfast in a couple violent heaves.

Mr. Sif removed both testes and tossed them into an enamel wash basin, then doused inside the wound with iodine and thickly coated the empty scrotum with coal tar to help prevent infection. Champ swung the pig back over the fence and released him.

"You boys go ahead and get the next one ready," Mr. Sif instructed as he walked over to the fence where Henny remained bent over the top rail.

"You okay?" he asked.

"Ja, I vill be okay. I'm sorry."

"Didn't you ever have to fix animals back home?"

"No, I've never seen that. I guess it happened on the farm, but I did not see an animal castrated."

"But I've even heard tell that the Natzis castrate prisoners in Poland."

"I don't know if that is true, but Wilhelm Shingler says that it was done. One of the guards at Norway Camp is a Jew man who does not conceal his hostility to us. Shingler talks at night about castrating him just as he had seen Jews castrated in Poland. He said that he had helped select Jewish prisoners to be sterilized by x-rays. After several days they would swell up and some would be cut out. Shingler may just be talking. I have not heard it from anyone other than him."

Minutes passed as Henny's words were absorbed by the now-quiet workers. Mr. Sif finally broke the silence with, "We got ta git on. You come on back when you straighten up."

"Git, you mangy hound," Champ interrupted, throwing a stick at Judas, who had grabbed one of the testes and run under the wagon.

"Don't let 'em take yo' supper, Champ," Mr. Sif yelled.

"I'll break his back if he come over heah again."

"C'mon, you jacklegs. You just standin' 'round. Git 'nother shoat up heah," Mr. Sif instructed, trying to get his workforce organized again. "Anticipation. That is what you got to learn. You need to be one step ahead o' the man you're helping. Now you oughtta be able to do that. Anticipation!"

An event that was usually marked by banter and frivolity turned somber. The balance of the morning moved slowly. After the last boar had been castrated, Champ wrapped the testes in old newspaper and put them under the wagon seat.

Sif and Henny washed off on the back porch, then went inside for dinner with Granny Jack. Sugarbread and I stayed outside and ate with Champ under the oak tree.

While we were eating, Mr. Tindall made a stop at the mailbox and continued on toward Norway. Sugarbread and I raced to the road to get the mail and raced back, collapsing against the front of Mr. Sif's pickup.

"Beat ya," said Sugarbread, who was squeezing one of his hands within the other. Then, looking around at the front of the pickup, he cried, "I cut my hand!"

Champ looked over and saw the broken headlight at the same

time we did. "Now, look what you kids done to that lamp."

"Naw, suh," responded Sugarbread, "we ain't did nuttin. We just leaned up 'ginst de truck."

"That lamp's been shot out," I informed Champ. "There's buckshot holes all 'round the fender."

"Well, you come on away from there. Let me see how bad yo' hand is." Champ beckoned to Sugarbread.

"It ain't bad at all, it just stings a little," Sugarbread replied, holding the cut finger between his britches legs. He screamed, briefly, as Champ put a few drops of the iodine from Mr. Sif's bottle on the cut.

"Now you hush up, acting like somebody be killin' you."

Conflicting images began a tug of war to win my mind. This could explain a lot. Mr. Sif was a Ku Klux Klanner and probably the leader. But he would never have burned a cross in front of Granny Jack's place. He couldn't be a Klanner. Yet there it was, as clear as anything could be, buckshot in the fender and headlamp. *There's good reason he don't tell nobody about his past*, I thought.

When Granny Jack and Mr. Sif came outside, I said nothing about the headlamp.

"What was all that screaming about out heah?" Mr. Sif asked.

"Sugarbread just cut his hand, but it's okay now," I assured him.

"Well, let's git going on those troughs."

Mr. Sif's carpentering was strictly utilitarian. With thick boards of green lumber and some tin strips, he could fabricate nearly anything that need demanded. He prided himself in the fact that his joints always stayed together—wrapping each joint with a narrow band of tin secured with a couple of ten-penny spikes assured that. Green wood held a nail well, and the band kept the boards from splitting as they dried. The weight alone added to their stability and discouraged both theft and borrowing. No one called on Mr. Sif to make household furniture, but his talents were counted on when barns or troughs or porch benches were needed.

Champ unloaded the rest of the boards from the wagon and placed them on the sawhorses for Mr. Sif to measure and cut.

Champ usually had little to say, but I thought he was quiet that afternoon. If he made the connection between the broken headlamp and the incident the night before, he made no suggestion of it.

The argument raged on in my mind. I leaned a short two-by-twelve against the front of Mr. Sif's pickup to cover the broken headlamp. I stared at Mr. Sif all afternoon, being convinced one moment that his bird-like figure was a vulture and knowing in the next moment that he was exactly who and what Granny Jack knew him to be.

Sugarbread and I wrestled with the heavy hog troughs, placing them in the pens after the men nailed them together. Anticipation had little chance of occupying my thoughts. That is, until Granny Jack said in my direction, "Take that board from against Mr. Sif's truck." Noting my hesitance, she repeated, "Well do as I say boy, he don't have time to fool around with you." Reluctantly, I pulled away the board and tried unsuccessfully to block the view of the shot-riddled fender with my body.

"Is that lamp broken? Will, did you break that lamp?"

Granny Jack had plenty of reason to be suspicious. She knew I had thrown rocks at Mr. Sif's pickup on more than one occasion when I didn't get my way.

"Nawsum, Miz Jack," Champ interrupted, "I done asked him dat. Dat lamp's been shot out."

"Oh my God, not you Sif!" Granny Jack cried as she turned on him. "How could you, you son of a bitch! Git off my place!" She pounded at his chest with both fists.

"Hold on Jack, what on earth are you talking about? It's my truck, ain't it? What's it got to do with you?"

"I shot this lamp out last night when you were out here with the Klan and those hoods."

"Jack, I didn't go nowhere last night, but I reckon I know who did. My Alec used the truck last night to go drinking with his friends."

Mr. Sif's words brought an end to Granny Jack's anger, but everyone's discomfort at seeing the two old friends at odds with each other forced them away from the scene and back to the pig lot. Even at a distance we could hear Mr. Sif promise, "He'll be back heah befo' sundown, this time to git straight."

But Alec did not come back that afternoon. He had returned to Fort Jackson early in the day. We saw him no more that summer.

When winter came, the stumps in the back field that Mr. Sif had planned to dynamite that afternoon were still in the ground. Champ kept the dynamite ready in the corner of the hayloft in anticipation of the time Mr. Sif would say, "Reckon we oughta shoot those stumps in the back field tomorrow."

I wondered if Henny had ever cleared stumps at his farm in Germany.

# CHAPTER SIXTEEN

The *Times and Democrat*, Saturday August 26. "Paris Radio Asserts Capital Liberated"

Supreme Headquarters, Allied Expeditionary Force. August 25—(AP)—The Paris radio announced late tonight that the French capital had been liberated and that the German commander had signed a document ordering his troops to cease fire immediately.

The announcement followed entry of American and French troops into the capital during the day. . . .

Gen. Charles de Gaulle, president of the French Committee of National Liberation said in a speech broadcast from Paris:

"France will take her place among the Great Nations which will organize the peace. We will not rest until we march, as we must, into enemy territory as conquerors. . . ."

In another broadcast the Paris radio said that the German commander had signed the following document, presented by Brig. Gen. Jacques Le Clerc, commander of the French Second Armored Division and leader of the French force which entered the capital during the day:

"The German commander gives orders to the forces under his command to cease fire immediately. Arms are stacked. . . ."

Tonight's announcement followed bitter fighting in the heart of the capital by French and American armored forces of the U. S. Third Army which rolled in this morning. . . .

In the fog of early morning, American infantry—the first of this second American expeditionary force within a generation to enter Paris—battled to Notre Dame, whose ancient bells a few hours before had welcomed the first French patrols to the city.

On all sides the liberating French and Americans were greeted by hungry Parisians, mad with joy, who had fought alone against the German oppressors since they were called to arms last Saturday. . . .

Men, women, and children lined the path of the Allied advance, and Whitehead said that when his column stopped, he was all but smothered by Frenchmen swarming around his jeep.

Said one old man, saluting with tears in his eyes, "God bless America. You have saved France."

* * *

As the cotton bolls burst under the August sun, a great white smile swept across the fields surrounding Champ's house. Granny Jack walked the rows every day in anticipation of the morning she would send for "her POWs" to begin picking. By the first week in September, she was ready for the full crew and sat with Henny on the porch steps awaiting the PW truck.

"What do you plan to do when the war is over?" Granny Jack asked.

Henny hesitated, staring blankly at the step beneath his feet, then slowly pulled a tattered scrap of paper from his wallet and handed it to Granny Jack.

"You know I can't read it, Henny. What does it say?" she asked.

"I'm sorry Miss Jack, it's my notice about Erick. I received it after ve arrived in Africa."

"We regret to inform you," he read from the paper, "of the death of your beautiful son Erick in the early morning hours of November 3, of pneumonia. His doctors worked valiantly, but in the end could not save him from this fulminant infection. Because of the continuing threat of epidemic, his remains have been cremated. In your absence, Erick's personal effects will be delivered to Frau Stauss in Berlin. Any inquiries should be addressed to this institution in writing, visits for the present being forbidden as part of police precautions against infection.

"Please accept our deepest sympathy. Signed Dr. Fritz Morgen, medical officer, Eichberg Provincial Sanitorium and Nursing Home."

"Henny, I'm sorry. I didn't know you had a son. Do you have other children?"

"Nein, only Erick. He was like your Vill, blonde hair and skinny. Ve did not wish to have another child so soon when ve saw his problems. Then the war took me away and ve had no time."

"Tell me about your wife and Erick."

Henny had left the authority of school officials in 1934 to enter the apprentice work force, foregoing gymnasium by choice, perhaps influenced by family precedent and pressure. The Stauss family had provided reasonably for themselves on a small parcel of farmland and forest between Darmstadt and the Rhine River. Joseph Stauss perceived that industry was absorbing more of the country's manpower and that eventually, mechanized equipment would be necessary to take over the farming labor. He pushed Henny to pursue an apprenticeship to learn the workings of machines and electricity. When the land passed to Henny, he would be well prepared to manage the operation.

In the course of his apprenticeship, Henny gravitated away from the influence of his family, advancing—along with a growing number of Germany's fourteen-year-olds—into Hitler Youth proper. Membership in youth groups had swept through Europe after the Great War, attracting both sexes from farmland and city, rich and poor. Control of the direction of juvenile enthusiasm, idealism, energy, and even aggression, was an early goal of the Third

Reich. Transformation of various religious, recreational, and service groups into political, nationalistic, militaristic Hitler Youth organizations was well along by the mid-thirties. Only the Catholic Youth remained as a separate organization, but they too would be engulfed by the movement later in the decade. By the time Hitler took over Czechoslovakia as a prelude to wider aggression in Europe, almost everyone between ten and eighteen years of age served in some part of the Fuehrer's youth organizations.

Henny acknowledged his enthusiastic participation. Hitler captured his heart and his energy and his imagination. He came to the Hitler Youth movement already firm and agile from a childhood of constant work on the farm and easily mastered the athletic and marching requirements. He reveled in the ideal of being "tough as leather, swift as a greyhound, and hard as Krupp steel."

He participated with equal eagerness, whether collecting metal or paper for charity, learning vehicle repair, or practicing small arms drills. He loved the competitions, gymnastics, and war games. His greatest satisfaction came not from individual achievements but from being lost in the massive, uniformed assemblages that marched, chanted, and performed athletic feats before a reviewing stand of Nazi officers.

He lived for the opportunities to see and hear his Fuehrer. "You, my youth, are our nation's most precious guarantee for a great future, and you are destined to be the leaders of a glorious new order under the supremacy of National Socialism. Never forget that one day you will rule the world!"

"Seig Heil! Seig Heil! Seig Heil!" Henny had strained with the multitude of youth at every break in Hitler's delivery.

Henny moved into the Hitler Youth proper at a time when the movement was shedding its earlier reputation as a reservoir of undisciplined and poorly educated rowdies. Although members continued to embark on missions of harassment or destruction at the slightest encouragement, the officers became more demanding in their rules of deportment and duty.

"When I was almost eighteen, our unit vas railed to Nuremberg for a rally with over 100,000 other Hitler Youth and members of The League of German Girls from throughout the Reich. It was the first time ve used forged papers to get into the beer houses and cinemas. I supplied a large number of the counterfeit papers for other youth with the knowledge of the officers. The girls were not interested in anyone without the papers. I met Kari at that rally."

Henny's return to Darmstadt was greeted with receipt of his long-awaited assignment to the elite Motorized Hitler Youth. He departed immediately for Frankfurt for enrollment, an event that had delayed his knowledge of Kari's pregnancy.

He'd acknowledged possible paternity for the unborn child when confronted by a team of officers tasked with seeking the Hitler Youth members responsible for the 900 pregnancies that had been initiated during the course of the six-day Nuremberg rally. Nazi headquarters had come under increasing criticism because of the numbers of girls who were being impregnated during league activities. While the bearing of a "child for the Fuehrer" within the bonds of wedlock was encouraged, it was by no means frowned upon officially for those with pure ancestry to do so beyond these bounds. Nevertheless, in order to quiet the complaints from the pregnant girls' parents, some effort was made to establish the identity of the fathers and to encourage marriage. In this instance, their job, an undertaking that would eventually turn up less than half the fertile youth involved, was made easy. Henny took steps immediately to have the child born within marriage and gained means of support by enlisting in the army.

The gestation proceeded mostly in Henny's absence at the home of Kari's parents in the southern outskirts of Berlin. He managed an occasional visit during basic training but maintained contact mostly by telephone.

Doctor Brandt had pronounced Erick "the picture of Aryan beauty" at birth and during his examination at four weeks old.

In retrospect, Kari sensed that something was wrong from the beginning. She hesitated to voice her concerns except to Henny, fearing that it might unleash a flood of guilt and further alienate her parents, who had been slow to accept her pregnancy and her marriage. She was reassured only briefly by the pronouncement of health and beauty at each visit to see the nurse or Doctor Brandt. As Erick approached nine months, he was unable to sit with his own strength and made no effort to crawl. His joints appeared less supple and his muscles more taut with each passing week. His growth followed a mediocre course, although he seemed to nurse well and accommodated an adequate volume of breast milk.

Kari's mother attributed the problem to weakness in Kari's milk. She brooded about what the Reich was doing to motherhood. It wasn't appropriate, she maintained, for the girls to be marching and performing gymnastics, activities that kept them from rounding out their bodies and so diminished their ability to carry and nourish young. She viewed the Fuehrer's superbaby farms as a sham.

"Superbabies, shahh! They're put there because their mothers can't nurse them. You don't see the wetnurses there slim and lean like soldiers going off to war." Frau Linden was amply rounded, an apt example of what she considered to be the proper physiognomy for motherhood. Her well-intentioned dissection of Erick's problems edged Kari further toward depression at a time when she was already burdened with growing guilt and a sense of futility in trying to help her son—or even understand what was wrong.

Henny had given his full support to Kari when she decided to be more forceful in demanding an explanation during the next visit with Dr. Brandt.

"I know something's wrong," she blurted out immediately, tears welling in her eyes and overflowing. "I know you've told me he's okay, but something's wrong."

Doctor Brandt appeared relaxed, free of any sign of being pressed by an anteroom crowded with infants and children in various stages of ill health or the desk behind him laden with uneven stacks of unread articles, unfinished charts, and unanswered notes, several topped with half-smoked pipes as if to limit the accumulation of additional work that could not be completed. The general clutter of the office contrasted sharply with his personal appearance, lean and neatly groomed, finished with a vest and tie. A sandy mustache softened a rawboned face and added some years to his age. His relaxed manner and toleration of the condition of his office befitted a man much heavier.

"Let me see how he's doing. You know it's easy to put too much pressure on yourself with Henny away. It's easy to get things out of perspective."

"Maybe so," Kari acknowledged. "I hope that's it. But I worry about his feet," she continued, fondling the tiny stiff feet. "I worry about his back, and Momma is driving me crazy. She says it's all my milk."

"Do you think he sees okay?"

"He seems to. Yes, I'm sure he does. He watches the squirrels in papa's backyard."

"Does he follow sounds?"

"Yes, I think he hears everything around."

"Can he tell you from other people?"

"Definitely. Just try to hold him for a few minutes."

"Tell me about his feeding."

"He nurses strongly and seems satisfied. Momma thinks that's the problem—that it's my milk. But that's not what concerns me. He's just not doing right. He's not as attentive as he used to be. He can't do the things he ought to be doing. He can't even sit up by himself yet. And this odor," she added. "His odor saturates everything. His entire room smells like this."

"I'm afraid I can't help you with odors. Doctors become immune to offensive odors early in training. What little smell I had left has been done in by that pipe."

"Well, he's a handsome baby, Kari," Doctor Brandt offered as he began inspecting apertures and appendages and listening here and there. "He does seem a little stiff. And you say he doesn't try to sit up by himself yet?"

"He hasn't shown any interest in sitting yet."

"How long has this rash been present?"

"It comes and goes. I guess he's had some off and on for a couple months. Is that where the odor comes from?"

"I wouldn't think so. Eczema shouldn't cause any odor. It will probably come and go on its own schedule later in childhood."

His examination complete, Doctor Brandt concluded that Erick seemed a bit behind but not so much as to cause him undue concern. "Could the family be doing too much for him?"

"We do everything for him. Are you telling me that he's just lazy?"

"I guess not. We do see that from time to time, but usually in later babies. If that's all it is, he'll tire of it soon and will be into everything. I could probably get a consultation with Doctor Conti at the hospital if you wish. He's a specialist in children's diseases. He could probably give us some reassurance."

"When could we see him?"

"It will probably take several months. Maybe by then he will be making some progress."

But the consultation brought neither reassurance nor any measure of comfort to Kari. Doctor Conti found Erick to be severely delayed in development, probably of heritable cause, and likely to worsen with time. He took little time in recommending that Erick be taken to the sanitorium in Munster where the staff were prepared to provide care for damaged children.

John Linden, Kari's father, was cold and reasoning in the matter. "It's better to put him away. I've seen it before. The Shaws had a child that was an idiot and it destroyed the whole family. It won't ever come to no good."

"Now, John, you can't blame the problems in that family on the child. The family wasn't right before the child came."

"Say what you want, Anna, but they're better off with their own kind. And Kari will be better off, too. When a child's not right, there's no reason to try to keep him in a normal home. The fatherland provides for these children."

Over the ensuing months, Kari became paralyzed with grief and depression, her world withdrawing to the inside of the Linden house and to a small walled garden outside the kitchen. Radio and newspapers assaulted her fragile sense of worth, which called for strength and commitment that she did not have. Anna Linden assumed the care of Erick—she carried him for outings in the park, bathed him and prepared his clothes, and arranged for his visits to the clinic. She also prepared the application for admission to the Munster Sanitorium, which Kari signed without resisting. Henny had consented to the placement as a temporary measure until the war was over and he could retake control of the matters of his family.

On Henny's first visit to Munster after Erick's admission, he was impressed by the expansive facilities and friendly workers. The grounds were beautifully laid out and manicured; an ample staff appeared busy attending to every need of the children. Anna Gildebourg, the nurse in charge of Erick's ward, chattered continuously as she fluttered about, touching the children, rearranging toys, and directing attendants. Henny was overwhelmed by the variety and severity of afflictions he encountered in Erick's ward. Some, like Erick, appeared perfectly formed but with minds locked in an infantile state. Others had heinously malformed faces or limbs, in addition to mental defects. In a way, they all seemed content with the lot they had drawn in life.

Leave to spend even a few hours with Erick or Kari came with less frequency as the wheels of the German juggernaut crushed through Europe. Fingers of the daunting war machine extended into the Balkans, Russia, Scandinavia, and North Africa. Conscripts from conquered lands were taken to control and extend the vast and diverse empire. It was a Czechoslovakian conscript assigned to Henny's unit who first gave him cause for concern about Erick's safety.

"When the soldiers came through Brno, the old people and sick people who could not hide were shot or carried away in trucks. A boy's home was located on the road beyond the house of my parents. The soldiers moved in, and we heard only shots and saw covered trucks leaving. By the following day, the army had converted the house into an interrogation site," the Czeck reported.

Henny tried to ignore talk that residents of sanitoriums and other institutions back home in Germany also were being eliminated to diminish the drain of nonproductive individuals on the wartime economy. He reassured himself that it was only rumor. The doctors and nurses he had encountered in Munster certainly wouldn't stand for it. But with Erick's safety pressing on his mind, he decided to go to Munster to check firsthand. He arrived unannounced and was received graciously by Frau Gildebourg and Doctor Krieck.

"Sergeant Stauss, we are so glad to see you. Erick has been ill with a minor throat infection. We've had no sulfur for treatment, but he seems to have recovered very quickly on his own. With the institution being so poor, we've been managing him without writing you. Let's go find Erick. You will be glad to know that he has not had a seizure in several months."

The hospital appeared the same as on prior visits: immaculately kept, and the staff as attentive as they had always been. Frau Gilli, a gargantuan woman, was her usual jolly self, the wide space between her upper teeth showing through a broad smile. As she shuffled along with the men, she snapped the elastic of her girdle and rearranged the layers of her midsection. On seeing her, Henny was embarrassed at allowing even the possibility of mistreatment of children to enter his head.

Erick was found in his ward playing on the floor with six other boys. Henny thought he had seen them all before and remembered two by name. He thought the entire group would look more appropriate kicking a soccer ball in the park than in the confinement of an institution. Erick arose quickly upon seeing his father and threw his arms around him. The musky odor that had always been in his hair seemed less noticeable that day.

Henny and Erick walked over the grounds that afternoon hand and hand, smiling at other children and occasionally throwing a stone over the fence enclosing the institution grounds. As on Henny's previous visits, a scattering of other parents was there as well. Nothing gave any suggestion of so sinister an undertaking as gassing helpless children.

On leaving, Henny would again be reassured briefly by Doctor Krieck. "I've been distressed by the rumors of the insane and the retarded being put to death. What do you know of this?"

"Oh, we have heard these same rumors, too, Sergeant Stauss. The Jews and enemies of the Fuehrer have taken advantage of the emotion that can be aroused by such rumors.

"Our staff is devoted to these children and grow very fond of them, unfortunately more so than some of their parents. We grieve when any child dies. You may be assured that I personally investigate each death of one of our children."

"To be sure," Frau Gildebourg interrupted, "we have children die here—nearly every week. But even that is improved now with the transfer of so many to institutions closer to their homes. We are finally getting down to a number we can care for."

"I'm reassured to see Erick so happy and in such good hands. Kari will be pleased to have such a good report. It will have a good effect on her."

And indeed, it did. Kari had suffered long with the idea of Erick entering Munster Sanatorium in the first place. She would never have consented if Henny were still at home. But with him involved in the war, it was clear that she could not physically handle Erick, particularly when he had seizures. She was excited that Henny had seen Erick and could bring good news.

"Oh Henny, tell me all about him."

"Erick is fine," Henny had reported. "I saw him and all his roommates. Frau Gilli and Doctor Krieck still take care of him. He looks well."

"Could he talk? Is he learning new things?"

"He is very much the same, except he is growing. You would be happy to see how big he is now. But he still doesn't say any words. And he hasn't had any seizures at all. They give him a new medicine for his seizures," Henny added.

"Oh, I'm so glad he's okay. You hear so much in the streets."

"Well, he is in good hands. There are always rumors during a war. We will go to see him together when I return next from France."

Kari seemed relaxed for the first time since Erick had been placed at Munster two years before. They sat together by the fire and ate there. She was playful, buoyed by Henny's visit to Erick and having her husband beside her. They were both forgetful of the war.

Nearly three months passed, during which Henny took only one brief leave when Kari met him in Paris. On October 3, Kari called him in a hysterical state. Erick had been transferred to Eichberg Sanitorium. A terse note had arrived, stating that the transfer was necessary because of the wartime circumstances, and was stamped with Doctor Krieck's signature.

"Oh Henny, I knew something was going to happen to him. I could feel it."

"Now, Kari, I'm sure there is some explanation. I will ring Doctor Krieck today. You go to your parents' home and I will call you there later."

It was hours before Henny could get through, but eventually Frau Gildebourg was on the line.

"Much to his own displeasure, Doctor Krieck was reassigned to an army unit a fortnight ago. The letter that you and Kari received was stamped with his name since no replacement has arrived here yet. It has broken my heart to see those children leave, but it is for the best. I am sure good and kind care will be given to Erick at Eichberg Sanitorium. We are now receiving tuberculous patients here."

"Do you know any of the people up there?"

"Not personally—our people have been assigned to other camps. All the children were sent by bus under the conveyance of the German army to a Doctor Morgen."

Henny's mind was again consumed by the rumors of mercy killings as he entered his commander's office. "Heil Hitler!" He saluted after coming to attention with a click of his heels.

"Heil Hitler!" responded Captain Huber. "You may be at ease, Sergeant Stauss."

"I have just received news of the transfer of my child to Eichberg Sanitorium. I would like to request a pass to check on his safety and that of my wife."

"My dear Stauss, you are too much consumed by your family at home. We are involved in a war. We may be moving any day now to cross the channel and occupy England."

"But—a few days and I shall return," Henny pleaded.

"I am afraid it is not possible, Stauss. You have taken leave twice since July," Huber noted, flipping through Henny's dossier. "Let me speak more directly, Stauss. You have taken a wife whose mother is Polish. That is bad enough. Having a child who is a burden to the fatherland is too much. But then, one might expect one to follow the other."

"My wife is Aryan."

"With a Polish mother? A name like Wachowski? Come now, Stauss."

"Kari and her family are totally devoted to the fatherland."

"Yes, but they are Polish. How can the fatherland be pure? You can see what happened with her first child."

"Our first child . . ."

"Now Stauss, you're a good man. Why don't you avoid a lot of trouble for yourself? Why don't you forget about your Polish wife and make a new life, an Aryan life for yourself. There will be no pass. You are dismissed. Heil Hitler!"

Within a week, Henny had been transferred to another infantry division heading south to strengthen Kesselrin's Tenth Army, charged with holding northern and central Italy. He was captured along Route 7 between the Alban Hills and Rome following a minor shrapnel wound to the right thigh. Along with others taken in General Clark's push toward Rome, Henny was transshipped to Tunisia and from there to the United States. Within weeks of arriving in the States, he was interred at Camp Norway . . . and soon after would become the object of my curiosity.

# CHAPTER SEVENTEEN

The *Times and Democrat.* "World Series Opens Today at Sports-man's Park, St. Louis. Mort Cooper pitted against Galehouse in First Contest." October 4, 1944.

St. Louis, October 4—(AP)—The first All-St. Louis World Series in the 41-year history of the baseball classic opens tomorrow with the Cardinals' Mort Cooper, ace of the National League champions' staff, opposing veteran Dennis Galehouse, surprise nominee of the Browns.

Manager Billy Southworth's selection of Cooper to get the Cards away in front in the best four-out-of-seven series was in line with the big righthander's 22 and 7 record during the season.

But the naming of the 32-year-old Galehouse caught this baseball-wild city by surprise. Luke Sewell, pilot of the surging Browns, had been expected to lead off with Nelson Potter, leading hurler on his staff with a 19-7 record. . . .

Cooper has not pitched since beating the Phillies in a 16-inning affair 10 days ago. He kept in shape, howev-er, by working out every day of the Cards' final week in the East. He said today he was in fine fettle. Galehouse's last outing was Saturday when he blanked the New York Yankees 2 to 0 on five hits. . . .

As the result of the argument, which has split this town wide open, 35,000 or more fans are expected to be in compact Sportsman's Park when Umpire Ziggy Sears yells "Play Ball" at 2 p.m. (Central War Time). All of the reserved seats have been sold for days. Seven thousand unreserved seats will go on sale at 10 o'clock tomorrow morning. The bleacher line started forming this morning with a 17-year-old St. Louis boy first in line at 8:15 a.m.

\* \* \*

Cotton production on Granny Jack's farm in 1944 fell shy of her goal of one bale per acre. The lint, however, brought twenty-one cents per pound, a record high and more than twice the sale price in 1940. The ledgers at Chaplin Brothers' and Livingston's Mercantile were cleared; Champ received good faith money for the purchase of clothes and shoes. For the first time in over a decade, money was put in reserve for the next season. Granny Jack held uncashed allotment checks from four sons in the military. The strong cotton market and encouraging news from the European and Pacific fronts brought the town to the Harvest Baseball Game brimming with optimism.

Even so, a trace of mutual mistrust remained in the air. The Baptists were still miffed about last year's match-up. Game day the previous year fell on a weekend when Alec Tyler had been home on leave from Fort Jackson. In his company was a contingent of fellow troops from his barracks, who'd mauled the Baptists. The Baptists had cried foul but acknowledged the tradition that allowed visitors to a church member's home to play in the annual event. Nonetheless they'd smoldered all year over the issue, eventually negotiating a rule with the Methodists that no one who lived outside the county, even if they were the guest of a church member, would be eligible to play.

A full year of argument and clarification of the rules had intervened as church leaders from both sides sought assurances that last year's atrocity would not be repeated. To prevent escalation of a recruiting war, they further eliminated loopholes used frequently by both sides in the past, including enlistment of young men from other churches, visiting ministers and missionaries, and young men who came to church during September solely to qualify for the October contest.

As usual, the Methodists arrived first, coming directly from morning services, and spread the bounty of their gardens and kitchens on a long line of tables. Baptist preaching and singing always took longer and did not yield even for occasions of this magnitude. The gastronomic contest between Baptists and Methodists began one hour before the Harvest Game, continued throughout and well beyond the nine innings, and was as celebrated as the events on the field.

At last, a parade of mule-drawn wagons, pickups, and cars brought the Baptists through the pecan grove and onto the school's grounds. An onslaught of hugging and kissing ensued among the adult belligerents. The Baptist women interspersed their blue-tagged baskets and bowls and platters among those already set out by the Methodists. Henny helped me place apple pies sent by Granny Jack on the dessert table before returning to the wagon where Enno and Frederick stood surveying the crowd. Frederick was not among the initial four POWs that came to Granny Jack's farm in April but occasionally substituted for one of them. The wonderful mix of aromas from meat and vegetables and desserts permeated the grounds.

Mr. Sif gave several blasts on a turkey call and announced that the Reverend Bates would invoke the "blessings of the Lawd" on the festivities of the day.

"Here we are, Lord. Laborers in your vineyard. Endowed with your rich earth, warmed by your sun, enlivened by your showers, refreshed by your winds. Gatherers of your plenty. Thank you, Lord. Thank you, Lord.

"Here we are, Lord. Mothers and fathers and sisters and brothers of many who are strung out around this vast world. We thank you for the fighting men who must bring this world to right. We thank you for the women who have stepped up to take their places here at home. Keep them safe, Lord, keep them safe.

"Here we are, Lord. Your disciples in a world . . ." Bates continued his litany of thanks.

What turned out to be an uncharacteristically brief prayer was greeted by a chorus of "Amens!" and a rush of young children to the first of the serving tables. I introduced Jake Hutto to Henny and Enno and Frederick and the five of us tossed Jake's baseball about as we waited for the crush at the tables to diminish. Several young men were loosening their pitching arms on the grassy field. A few colored folks were beginning to gather beyond the outfield. Aaron Sligh was busy at the back of his wagon, trying to tune in WIS on a battery radio to keep track of the fourth game of the World Series, which was scheduled to begin at three o'clock.

A few unfamiliar faces were being escorted through the crowd and introduced. As my guests and I started along the food tables, they were greeted cordially and welcomed to this show of Americana.

"I'm Miz Hattie Padgett. This is my chicken pie over here. Make sure to get a good helping and come back for some more."

"It's so nice to meet you. James and I—that's him over there with Preacher Bates—we've got two boys in the war. My blackberry pie's down there with a blue ribbon. I'm sure you'll enjoy a good piece of it if it ain't already gone."

"We're so glad to have you men with us today. I've been meaning to get over to your camp with some books but just haven't got around to it. Don't miss a slice of my cured ham down on the next table."

"Let me help you with some of my snap beans. My men could make a meal offa just them."

"I'm Preacher Lewis. We were glad to have you in church today. Look for my Bess's pickled okra. It is something good."

When the Methodists took to the field, Mr. Sif called the pitchers and catchers from both teams to home plate. He asked the preachers to join them with their lineups.

"I ain't gonna stand for no argument 'bout the calls today. For boys under thirteen and any girls, you pitch underhand and let 'em hit. If you pitch at 'em hard, I'm gonna put 'em on base. If you hit anybody, I'm gonna put 'em on base. You got to play everybody you got on ya' team least one full inning. Two extra boys or girls kin play in the outfield, but you gotta let 'em bat. Now, looks like the Methodists got a Junior Bowman from Pine Hill who's a guest of the Tindalls'. Where's this young man gonna be playing?"

"That's him out on third base," Preacher Bates responded. "He's dating that young Tindall girl and seems like one of the family."

"Don't see any problem with him. You got any objection?" Mr. Sif asked of Preacher Lewis.

"Looks like he qualifies by the rules."

"Now, heah on the Baptist list, you got these three prisoners," Mr. Sif continued.

"Yeah. They came to church with young Will Livingston and he says they're his guests. They live here in the county, and I couldn't see no grounds to keep 'em from playing. Besides, the Germans don't know how to play baseball. They oughta be fun to watch."

"Looks like it may be stretchin' the rules a little bit, but if Preacher Bates ain't got no objection, I'm gonna let 'em play."

"When I've been over to the camp, I ain't seen 'em do nothing but kick and butt that soccer ball around," Bates responded. "My pitchers will be able to take care of 'em."

Noodle Perry, the Methodist pitcher, had to wait until the third inning before getting a shot at the Germans.

On my way to a position between Henny and left field, I spotted Sugarbread and Champ and Tunia among the colored people who had come through the woods to watch the game from a knoll beyond the outfield. They were sharing baskets of food, which they spread out on quilts. I imagined their food was even more inviting than the bounty on our tables. I waved to Sugarbread, who had come to the front of their gathering.

"Hit one to me, Will," he called as we pegged a ball around the outfield and waited for the first batter.

We retired the first inning for the Methodists on a grounder to shortstop, a pop fly to short right field, and an infield popup with one man who had walked and stolen second left on base.

Noodle's variety of pitches tied our batters in knots. Nearly every contact drove the ball into the infield dirt and an easy out. In the second inning we got a man on base with a late swing that placed a blooper safely into right field, but he was caught in a double play to retire the inning.

Everyone with the slightest interest in the contest watched as Henny led off in the bottom of the third. He went for three straight pitches, hitting two foul balls and over-swinging Noodle's sinker by a foot.

Aaron Sligh got us started with a liner between first and second, which was bobbled by the right fielder, fired past second on the throw in, and rolled out of bounds, coming to lie between Pearl and Queenie. Aaron took third before Mr. Sif halted the game to retrieve the ball. Aaron came in on a wild pitch and our single run held until the fifth, when the Methodists posted a four-run rally on a series of Baptist errors in the outfield, including a double error by Henny and me.

I often think about that bright October afternoon. Colored men and children sat knotted together beyond left field, whooping as a ball skipped through Henny's legs and into the blackberry patch, cheering wildly when he hit one of Noodle's fast balls into their crowd, and finally disappearing into the woods when the last of the picnic was eaten and the last batter was out.

Women of many shapes in flowered cotton dresses, almost oblivious to the contest in progress, fanned flies from the near empty dishes and shared letters from their sons and daughters. Children raced about the perimeter, attracted momentarily by the solid crack of a good contact, running down foul balls, shooting marbles from a pig eye, climbing on the limbs of twin chinaberry trees, and paying repeated visits to the dessert table. Men with Camels or Lucky Strikes dangling on their lips sat atop car fenders and picnic tables and attended to every move from the plate to the outfield as they talked. Mr. Sif stood in the middle of it all, calling balls and strikes with absolute impartiality and wielding over the gathering his familiar, intangible control.

The adults knew that at this same moment, battles were raging from the Rhineland to Leleliu. Some of their sons and husbands and fathers would never come home. They saw the enemy on the field before them. They fed them, sat beside them, applauded their successes, laughed at their errors, and in the end hugged them before they headed back to Norway Branch Camp. The long task of healing the wounds of a war still being fought had begun.

Years would pass before I recognized that Sugarbread wanted only to be in the outfield beside me.

# ABOUT THE AUTHOR

**Roger Stevenson** spent the first decade of life on a cotton farm in South Carolina. There was a family expectation that he would go to college and medical school, as the mantel for this pursuit had passed to him from an uncle whose education had been sidelined by World War II.

His education and military obligation took him progressively farther north to Furman University (South Carolina), Wake Forest School of Medicine (North Carolina), Johns Hopkins Medical Center (Maryland), and the U.S. Air Force (Alaska). In 1974, he returned to his native state and founded the Greenwood Genetic Center and the Greenwood Children's Clinic. By this time, he had published his first medical book. Several editions of two other medical texts would follow. The Greenwood Genetic Center grew into an internationally recognized diagnostic and research institution.

Roger and wife Leslie have made Greenwood, SC, their home for the past fifty years. Their four daughters and their husbands have thrived in this small community, contributing expertise in architecture, education, horticulture, medicine, and law.